The Men Who Explained Miracles

Books by John Dickson Carr

THE MEN WHO EXPLAINED MIRACLES

Six Short Stories and a Novelette by

JOHN DICKSON CARR

Harper & Row, Publishers

New York, Evanston, and London

Some of the Stories in this volume originally appeared in ELLERY QUEEN'S
MYSTERY MAGAZINE—

"William Wilson's Racket"
"The Empty Flat"
"Invisible Hands" (under the title "Death By Invisible Hands")
"Strictly Diplomatic"
"All In A Maze" (under the title "The Man Who Explained Miracles")

"The Black Cabinet"
This story originally appeared in *Twenty Great Tales of Murder* published by
Random House.

Contents

DEPARTMENT OF
QUEER COMPLAINTS

William Wilson's Racket

Colonel March, of the Department of Queer Complaints, has entertained many an odd sort of visitor in his office at New Scotland Yard. But it is seldom that he entertains a visitor so socially distinguished as Lady Patricia Mortlake, only daughter of the Earl of Cray.

She burst in like a whirlwind, that pleasant spring morning two or three years ago. She almost snorted through her aristocratic nose. And this despite the fact that Lady Patricia was normally one of those languid ladies, with a bored blank eye and a sullen underlip, who would have made an ideal heroine for Mr. Coward.

"She refuses to fill up an official form, sir," Colonel March was told. "And she's got a blasted Pekingese with her. But she showed me a note from the Commissioner himself—"

"Send her up," said Colonel March.

Lady Patricia subsided into a chair in a whirl and flop of furs, nursing the Pekingese. As a famous beauty, she perhaps photographed better than she looked. It was a highly enamelled sort of beauty, and her jaw looked as hard as porcelain.

She found herself facing a large, amiable man (weight seventeen stone) with a speckled face, a bland eye, and a cropped moustache. He was teetering before the fire, smoking a short pipe; and Inspector Roberts stood by with a notebook.

"I want you to find him," Lady Patricia said crisply.

"Find him?" repeated Colonel March. "Find whom?"

"Frankie, of course," said Lady Patricia, with some impatience. "My fiancé. Surely you've heard of him?"

3

Light came to Colonel March. Any newspaper-reader will remember the political reputation which was being made at that time by the Right Hon. Francis Hale, youngest of the Cabinet Ministers. Francis Hale was young. He was rich. He was intelligent. He had a great future ahead of him.

Anything that could be said against him was, so to speak, to his credit. Francis Hale always did the correct thing, even to becoming engaged to the impoverished daughter of an impoverished peer. He was a teetotaller, a nonsmoker, and a man of almost painfully straitlaced life. Colonel March privately considered him a good deal of a stuffed shirt.

"As far as I'm concerned," said Lady Patricia coolly, "I'm finished with him. We've done everything for that man. Everything! The right people, the right places, the right contacts. And I do hope I'm broadminded. But when he turned up to make a speech at that Corporation banquet, tight as a tick and practically blind to the world—!"

Now it has been stated before that nothing ever surprised Colonel March. This, however, came close to it.

"And," continued Lady Patricia, flirting her furs, "when it comes to that red-haired hussy—actually carrying on with her in public —well, really!"

Colonel March coughed.

In fact, he covered his happy smile only just in time. To any normal human being there is something heartening, something wholly satisfying, about seeing any stuffed shirt go on the razzle-dazzle. The colonel was no exception to this rule. But he caught sight of her eye, and was silent. Lady Patricia Mortlake was no fool. Also, it struck him that she had rather a mean eye and jaw.

"I dare say you think this is all very funny?" she inquired.

"Not at all."

"And I dare say," she continued, opening her veiled eyes and cuddling the dog with dangerous quietness, "you wonder why this concerns the police?"

"Since you mention it—"

"But it would interest the police, I hope, to hear that Frankie has disappeared? Throwing his whole department into confusion at a critical time; to say nothing of the inconvenience to my parents and me? It would interest you to hear that he vanished out of that horrible office in Piccadilly, where heaven knows what has been happening?"

Colonel March regarded her grimly.

"Go on," he invited.

"He's been acting queerly," said Lady Patricia, "for over a month. Ever since he first saw this."

From under her coat she took out a copy of a famous literary weekly, of the conservative and highbrow order, and unfolded it. She turned to the advertisements. With the tip of a scarlet fingernail she indicated one advertisement printed in bold black type. It said simply:

William and Wilhelmina Wilson, 250A, Piccadilly. Nothing more.

"It's been appearing in only the best papers," the girl insisted. "And every time Frankie sees it, he seems to go off his head."

Colonel March frowned.

"What," he asked, "is the business of William and Wilhelmina Wilson?"

"That's just it! I don't know."

"But if they're in a legitimate business, they must be listed?"

"Well, they're not." Her upper lip lifted defiantly. "I know, because we've had a private detective after Frankie. The detective says they sell vacuum cleaners."

Though Inspector Roberts had ceased in despair to take notes, Colonel March betrayed only an expression of refreshed interest.

He continued to teeter before the fire, and puff at his short pipe.

"It started," she went on, "one afternoon when I was waiting for him in the car outside the House of Commons. He stayed behind on the steps, talking interminably to that dreadful Labour man What's-his-name. He simply *wouldn't* come on, no matter how many gestures I made. When he did condescend to join me, he looked at me in a queer way, and asked the chauffeur to stop at the nearest news agent's. There he got out and bought a copy of that paper."

She pointed.

"I couldn't tell what he was looking at. But I knew there was something wrong with him. I asked him if he couldn't take any interest in what I was doing for him. Even in the concert of chamber music I'd arranged for that night, where Julio's Trio was to render selections from the modern masters. And he said—"

"Yes?" prompted Colonel March.

"He said 'Damn and blast the modern masters.' It was too utterly tiresome, when Julio is *all* the rage this season."

"Indeed?"

"Then I caught him cutting out that advertisement from the paper. That wouldn't have mattered, and I forgot all about it. But only a week ago I caught him cutting it out again, this time out of *The Times*. So," explained Lady Patricia, "I decided to find out who this 'William and Wilhelmina Wilson' really were. I paid them a visit yesterday."

Her eyes took on a shrewd, speculative look.

"Whoever they are," she said thoughtfully, "they've got pots of money. I expected to find the office some dreadful little place: you know. But it wasn't. My dear man, it's in a big new block of offices opposite the Green Park. So businesslike: that's what I can't understand. You go up in a lift, and there's a big marble corridor and a ground-glass door with 'William and Wilhelmina Wilson' on it."

Her expression was now one of active fury, which she tried to conceal. As though remembering to be maternal, she lifted the Pekingese, shook it in the air, and cooed to it with pouted lips. The dog sneezed the hair out of its eyes, and looked bored.

"I opened the door," she said, "and there was a big waiting-room. Empty. Some rather good bronzes and etchings, too. I called out. I rapped on the table. But nobody answered. Just when I was wondering what to do, Flopit here . . . izzums, precious! . . . Flopit found another door, and began to bark."

She drew a deep breath.

"I opened *that* door. It was a big office, like a secretary's office. In the middle was a big flat-topped desk, with a swivel-chair behind it. In the chair sat Frankie, my Frankie. And on his lap, with her arms round his neck, sat a horrible red-haired hussy, about nineteen years old."

This time it was a near thing.

Colonel March's cough was so prolonged and strangled that a blind man would have noticed something wrong. Lady Patricia's hard eye noted it, and hated it. But she had to speak now.

"Well, really! I mean to say! I hope I'm broadminded, but—! My dear man, I was boiling; positively boiling. I didn't say anything. I just picked up Flopit by his precious neck, and walked out, and slammed the door. I walked across the waiting-room, and out into the hall.

"But I didn't go any farther. After all, I have Frankie's good at heart. And Frankie is awfully rich, and it didn't seem right that *she* should get his money, whereas I . . . I mean, when you've worked and slaved for a man, as I've worked and slaved for Frankie . . . well, it's rather thick.

"I waited in front of the door. Finally, I decided to go back and have it out with them. Back I marched into the waiting-room; and there I met somebody I hadn't seen before. A well-dressed elderly man. Rather distinguished-looking: bald except for white hair at the back of his head, curling down nearly to his collar.

"He said, 'Yes, madam?'

"I said, 'Who are you?'

"He said, 'I am William Wilson. Have you an appointment?'

"I just froze him. I asked to see Mr. Hale. He had the nerve to raise his eyebrows and say that Frankie wasn't there: that he had never heard of any Mr. Hale and didn't know what I was talking about. I said I also supposed he didn't know anything about a red-haired girl either? He looked surprised and said he imagined I must mean Miss Wilhelmina Wilson, his niece and secretary—think of it!—but he still knew of no Mr. Hale.

"Well, really, that was too much! I just walked past him and opened the door to the office where I'd seen Frankie before. Frankie wasn't there; but the red-haired girl was. She was standing in front of another little door, which led to a kind of cloakroom, and looking disgustingly guilty. I simply pushed her out of the way, and looked in. But . . ."

Lady Patricia Mortlake gulped.

"Yes?" prompted Colonel March.

"Frankie wasn't there," she said.

"He wasn't in the cloakroom?"

"He wasn't *anywhere*," returned the girl, lifting her shoulders. "There was only one other room, a big private office overlooking Piccadilly, on the fourth floor. He wasn't hiding anywhere, because I looked. And there's no way out of any of the offices except through the door to the main corridor, where I'd been standing. Frankie wasn't there. But his clothes were."

"*What?*" demanded Colonel March.

"His clothes. The suit he'd been wearing: with his watch, and notecase, and papers, and key ring, and the fountain pen I gave him for his birthday. They were hanging up in a locker in the cloakroom. Clothes, but no Frankie. And he hasn't been seen since. Now do you wonder why I'm here?"

Hitherto Colonel March had been listening with an indulgent air. Now his sandy eyebrows drew together.

"Let me understand this," he said in a sharp and rather sinister voice. "You mean he literally disappeared?"

"Yes!"

"He couldn't, for instance, have slipped out while you were examining the various offices?"

"Without his clothes?" asked Patricia unanswerably.

There was a silence.

"Frankie!" she almost wailed. "Of all people, Frankie! Of course I suppose he could have sneaked out. For that matter, he could have climbed out of a window and down the face of the building into Piccadilly. But in his underwear? Frankie?"

"Suppose he had another suit of clothes there?"

"Why?" asked Patricia, again unanswerably.

It is not often that Colonel March finds himself stumped, definitely left flat and up against it. This appeared to be one of the times.

"And what have you done since?"

"What could I do? He's not at his flat here, or at his place in the country. Not one of his friends, including his private secretary, seems to know where he is. I even tackled that dreadful Labour man he seems to have been so thick with recently; and I thought for a second he was going to burst out laughing. But even *he* swore he didn't know where Frankie was."

"H'm," said Colonel March.

"We can't make this public, you see. That would be dreadful. And so you're our last hope. Haven't you got any theory?"

"Oh, theories!" said Colonel March, waving a big arm irritably. "I can think of half a dozen theories. But they don't explain the main difficulty. Suppose any lurid theory you like. Suppose the mysterious William and Wilhelmina Wilson have murdered him and hidden his body. Suppose there is a sinister political conspiracy against him. Suppose Francis Hale has disguised himself and is masquerading as the distinguished-looking old gentleman with the white hair . . ."

Patricia sat up straight.

"A supposition," said the colonel grimly, "about as likely as any idea that he went walking about the streets in his underwear. But I repeat: suppose anything you like! It still won't explain what puzzles me most."

"Which is?"

"The profession of William and Wilhelmina Wilson," answered Colonel March. "Any ideas, Roberts?"

Inspector Roberts, shutting up his notebook, ruminated on this.

"Well, sir—" he began hesitantly.

"Yes, yes; go on!"

"Well, sir, the point seems to be this. Either Mr. Hale disappeared of his own free will, or else he didn't. It looks to me as though he didn't."

"Oh? Why not?"

"The personal effects," said Roberts. "The watch and the notecase and the rest of it. If you were going to do a bunk somewhere, wouldn't those be the very things you'd take with you? It isn't as though he were trying to stage a fake suicide, or anything like that. One minute he's comfortably in that office, with the young lady in his lap"—Roberts coughed, and looked swiftly away from their guest—"and the next he's gone. That's the part I don't like."

Colonel March grunted.

"And yet," pursued Roberts, "if that pair have managed to make away with him, I can't for the life of me see how or why. It's like something out of Edgar Allan Poe."

He broke off, for a curious expression crossed Colonel March's face: it was as though he had been hit across the back of the head with a club.

"Good lord!" he muttered, in a hollow voice like a ghost. "I wonder if that could be it?"

"If it could be what?" demanded Lady Patricia.

"The name," argued Colonel March, half to himself, "might be a coincidence. On the other hand, it might be most infernally apt: the seal of Wilson." He turned to Lady Patricia. "Tell me. Can Francis Hale hold his liquor?"

She stared back at him.

"I don't know what on earth you're talking about!"

"Yes, you do." The colonel was irritable. "You told me a while ago that Hale, in one of his fits of being fed up—ahem—in one of his more erratic moments, got tight at a Corporation banquet. What did he drink?"

His visitor set her jaw.

"Everything," she said. "Beginning with cocktails and going all the way through to brandy. He simply sloshed it down. My father was frantic."

"And how did it affect him? Hale, I mean?"

"They said he never made a better speech. He mixed up the pages in reading it; and, to anybody who really knew what the speech was about, it sounded *horrible*. But nobody noticed anything. They even seemed to like it: which was a mercy, because—"

Colonel March rubbed his hands together. He was utterly pleased and absorbed, with a smile which threatened to dislodge the pipe from his mouth. Then he went over and patted his guest on the shoulder.

"Go home," he said. "Go home, take an aspirin, and stop worrying. Inspector Roberts and I are going to call on the Wilsons. I have every reason to believe I see a way out of the difficulty. In fact, I think I can promise it, now that I am able to guess—"

"Guess what?" demanded Lady Patricia, lifting the dog and shaking it at him.

"The racket of William Wilson," said Colonel March.

A smooth-slipping lift took them up to the fourth floor of number 250A Piccadilly. A holy calm, as of a temple, pervaded these marble premises. The names *William and Wilhelmina Wilson* were printed on the ground-glass door in black lettering as discreet as a visiting-card. Motioning Inspector Roberts to precede him, Colonel March opened the door.

The waiting-room inside was softly lighted and carpeted. Magazines were scattered on a centre table for the convenience of those who waited; the point which racked Inspector Roberts's wits was what in blazes they were supposed to be waiting for. And behind the reception desk at the far end sat a small, sleek, trim young lady with red hair. She was glancing through a copy of a fashionable weekly.

"Miss Wilson?" said Colonel March.

"Yes?" said Miss Wilson with polite briskness.

"I should like to see your uncle."

Colonel March laid his official card on the desk.

For a few seconds Miss Wilson looked at it gravely, and then raised her head. If the notoriously frigid Francis Hale had fallen for Miss Wilson, Inspector Roberts for one did not blame him; she had blue eyes of a deceptive demureness, and a mouth of the sort called generous.

But if Roberts expected to see any sign of guilt or even nervousness, he was disappointed. What flashed across her face was a smile of almost unholy glee, which she instantly corrected.

"My uncle has been rather expecting you," she admitted. "Will you walk into our parlour?"

She led them through the secretary's office—with its famous desk and swivel-chair—to a third office overlooking Piccadilly. Here, behind another flat-topped desk, sat a stout old gentleman with the manners of a cardinal. His glossy bald head was set off by a fringe of white hair which curved down to the back of his collar. He wore pince-nez, through which he was studying a pile of large photographs. He welcomed his visitors courteously.

"As my niece says," he told them, "I have been rather expecting you." His mouth tightened. "Please sit down. You had better remain too, Wilhelmina, my dear."

"In that case," said Colonel March, "I'll come straight to the point. Of course, your name isn't really Wilson?"

Mr. Wilson looked pained.

"Naturally not. It is a trade name. A"—he waved his hand—"a flight of poetic fancy, if you like."

"Yes," said Colonel March. "That's what I thought, as soon as I guessed what your racket was."

Now Mr. Wilson seemed more than pained; he seemed hurt.

"Racket!" he protested. "My dear sir! No, no, no, no! That is too much. Profession, if you like. Business, if you insist. Yes: say a business, and on a large scale. After all, I am a modern man who has simply seen a modern need for those who can afford it. I supply that need. And there you are."

"Aren't you afraid I'll give you away?"

Mr. Wilson permitted himself a slight smile.

"Hardly. If you were to look in there"—he indicated a row of filing cases along one wall—"and see the names of some of my more illustrious clients, I hardly think you would talk of exposure. There is one client, for instance . . . but we must not be indiscreet." He returned to an old grievance. "Profession, yes. Business, yes. But racket? Really, now! On the contrary, I flatter myself that I am something of a public benefactor."

Inspector Roberts was a patient man. As Colonel March's assistant, he had to be. But there are limits to the human curiosity of even the best-trained subordinate.

"Sir," he suddenly cried, "I can't stand any more of this. Before

I go completely off my chump, will you tell me what this is all about? What's going on here? What *is* the fellow's racket? And why should he call himself Wilson?"

All three of them looked at him—Mr. Wilson with a reproving cluck of the tongue, Miss Wilson with a smile, and Colonel March with blandness.

"He calls himself William Wilson," replied Colonel March, "after the story of the same name. That story was written by Edgar Allan Poe, as you so helpfully suggested. You don't remember the story?"

"No, sir, I can't say I do."

"William Wilson," said Colonel March, "met himself."

Roberts blinked.

"Met himself?"

"He met his own image," explained Colonel March, settling back comfortably. "I rather admire Mr. Wilson here. He is the proprietor of a unique Agency. He provides doubles for eminent men and women in their unimportant public appearances, so that the real men can can stop at home and get on with their work."

Mr. Wilson leaned across the desk and spoke earnestly.

"You would be surprised," he said, "at the call there is for our services. Consider the life of a public man! While he should be at work, custom demands that he make endless public appearances, none of them in the least an iota of good. He makes interminable tours of inspection; he lays cornerstones; he addresses mothers' meetings. Few if any of the people he meets have ever seen him before, or will ever see him again. And a good double—!"

Mr. Wilson drew a deep breath, rather sadly.

"I fear the idea is not mine," he went on. "It was tried out a few years ago by a very eminent American. He simply could not stand all the handshaking."

Wilhelmina Wilson intervened loyally.

"But you were the only one who saw its commercial possibilities," she cried, and sat down on the edge of his desk as though to defend him. She somewhat spoiled the effect of this by winking at Colonel March.

"Thank you, my dear," said Mr. Wilson. He turned back to his guests.

"Our fees, of course, are considerable," he added apologetically. "But you have no idea of the difficulties. Once I had to send all the way to South Africa to get a passable double for . . . well, well, again we mustn't be indiscreet!" He closed his eyes and smiled happily. "Then there is the question of elocution, voice-training, and so on. On the whole, I am proud of my handiwork. The next time you go to a cinema and see a newsreel, watch very closely! You may see something that will surprise you."

Inspector Roberts was getting his breath back.

"Then Mr. Hale—" he began.

"Ah, yes," murmured the proprietor of the Agency, brushing his dry palms together and frowning at Colonel March. "Mr. Hale! I imagine you saw a discrepancy when Mr. Hale's double, a promising young actor named Gabriel Fisk, got drunk at that banquet?"

"A discrepancy," said Colonel March; "but probably not the discrepancy you mean. Wasn't that rather rash of him, by the way?"

"Perhaps," admitted Mr. Wilson sadly. "But the lesser of two evils. You see, we hadn't known that Mr. Hale's fiancée was to be present; otherwise we should not have risked it. So, in case Fisk made a bad slip of some kind, he had to have an excuse for making a slip. Mr. Hale is a notorious and genuine teetotaller. But then (I thought) even a teetotaller can change his mind."

Colonel March chuckled.

"He can change his mind," said the colonel. "What he can't change is his digestive system. He can't work his way through a huge wine list, from cocktails to brandy, without either becoming ill or going to sleep. In a man who has never taken a drink in his life, I submit that it's a physical impossibility. When I heard of

that little performance, I said to myself: 'It is magnificent; but it
isn't Hale.' And, speaking of his fiancée . . ."

Wilhelmina Wilson stiffened.

Throughout this conversation she had several times seemed on
the point of speaking. She still sat on the edge of her uncle's desk,
staring moodily at the toe of her slipper. When Colonel March
spoke, she looked at her uncle as though with appeal.

But Mr. Wilson remained unruffled.

"Ah, yes!" he said. "That unfortunate affair yesterday morning!"

"What was unfortunate about it?" the girl demanded, with sudden passion.

"Tush!" said her uncle, raising a gentle but admonitory fore-
finger. He looked distressed. "Colonel March, my niece is—im-
pulsive. Like her poor mother, my sister. And she is very fond of
young Gabriel Fisk.

"You understand now what happened, I hope? That suit of
clothes, with the notecase and watch and the rest of it, has nothing
to do with the case. It's a supernumerary. Mr. Hale provided us
with an exact duplicate of his possessions. I am an artist, sir, or I
am nothing. Neither the suit nor its contents has been worn for a
week. Fisk left it hanging there in the locker when he changed in
that cloakroom after appearing at the Muswell Hill Flower Show
last Tuesday week.

"Yesterday Fisk, in his ordinary clothes, came in for instruc-
tions. He and my niece—" Mr. Wilson coughed. "It was unfortunate that Lady Patricia Mortlake walked in when she did. Fisk,
of course, simply slipped out when her back was turned. Unfortunately, Lady Patricia is a strong-minded person. She ransacked the
place, found the suit, and suspected I hate to think what."

"And Hale?" asked Colonel March, without batting an eyelid.
"The real Hale? Where is he now?"

Again Mr. Wilson was apologetic.

"At his country place, with his head under the bed-clothes, until he can think up an excuse to explain his supposed conduct. Even if he tells the truth, I'm afraid Lady Patricia will not like it. And I shall probably—er—lose a client. Life," said Mr. Wilson, shaking his head, "is difficult."

"Yes."

"In any case, as I said before, you will respect our little secret? Our racket, as you prefer to call it?"

Colonel March got to his feet. Always an impressive figure, he now seemed to fill the room. He put on his soft hat at a more rakish angle than was seemly, and picked up his silver-headed stick. His speckled face was aglow.

"Candidly," he said, "I can't do anything else. You've got me. If I understand the situation, to show up this racket would be to wreck half the public reputations in England. We can't have that. The public demands to be deceived. By gad, it *shall* be deceived! So, if Miss Wilson vouches for the truth of this story—?"

"Yes," said the girl, with her eyes on the floor.

"Then there's nothing more to be said. Sir, good day to you!"

"And to you, Colonel March," beamed Mr. Wilson. "Wilhelmina, my dear, will you show these gentlemen out?"

Wilhelmina did show them out. Yet she did not appear to be happy about anything. For the first time her manner displayed a trace of nervousness. In the outer office she suddenly stopped, and whirled round on them.

"You old—" she began explosively, and then broke off to laugh; or cry—Colonel March was not sure which. "What are you thinking?"

"Thinking?" repeated Colonel March, with massive innocence.

"Yes, you were! You know you were! I could see it in your face. What's the matter? Don't you believe our story even now? I swear to you that that suit of clothes hasn't been touched for a week!"

"Oh, that?" said the colonel, as though enlightened. "I believe that."

"Then what is it? What were you thinking?"

"Well," said Colonel March, "since you ask, I was thinking about the dog."

"Dog?" she echoed blankly.

"Lady Patricia Mortlake's dog. An objectionable dog. But then I don't like Pekes." Colonel March reflected. "It had one quality, though, that I did notice. The dog Flopit took absolutely no interest in strangers. You could show it the whole personnel of Scotland Yard, and it never so much as opened an eye—let alone barking. It's the sort of dog which barks only when it scents or senses someone it knows very well. So, if it was Gabriel Fisk who was here with you yesterday, I only wondered why Flopit set up the clamour that drew Lady Patricia Mortlake's attention to you both."

While the blue eyes never left him, and an expression of impish animation survived even the embarrassed colour of her face, Colonel March added a last word.

"Stick to him," he advised in an even lower voice. "You'll be much better for him than that high-born shrew who's got his life planned out to the last musicale and reception."

"I've been in love with Frank Hale for a long time," the girl confessed. "But I thought it might be better for him if we said—"

"There's no reason for you and your uncle to lie in order to please her," said Colonel March. "As for Hale, there are still a few gleams of humanity in him. Under you, please God, he may yet develop into a statesman. Good afternoon, Miss Wilson. Come, Roberts. We must go and find some more queer complaints."

The Empty Flat

There it was, the confounded radio going again.

Chase put down his pen. For some minutes he had had a vague idea that there was a disturbance going on somewhere, and suddenly it broke into his thoughts with intolerable loudness from the flat below. A Study of the Royal Exchequer and its Custodians from 1660 to 1688 may not be a popular subject on which to be writing a thesis, but it requires concentration. Douglas Chase, Ph.D., F.R. Hist.S., poked his head out of a maze of books like a dazed turtle.

The simile is not altogether deserved. Douglas Chase was neither turtle nor worm, but an eminently serious-minded young man who had a job of work to do. This thesis—if he won the prize—meant a great deal to him. It meant a full professorship at an American university, and a salary amounting to nearly two thousand pounds a year. To an English scholar such a salary seemed incredible, and Chase wondered hazily what he would do with it if he got it; but there it was.

"I think your chances are very good," a colleague had told him that afternoon. "All the same, I wish we knew a bit more about K. G. Mills."

For the only serious competition seemed to come from a man named K. G. Mills. Chase had never met K. G. Mills, about whom, in fact, there was some element of mystery. But his attainments looked formidable; and among Chase's friends the very name of Mills had become a huge and legendary symbol of villainy. Now that concentration was most necessary to beat Mills, the tenant of the flat below had decided to let his radio run mad.

First of all Chase cursed the construction of modern flats. His own was a modest two-room affair on the first floor of a new block near Primrose Hill: a hive of raw red brick and white paint. Tenants had filled it like flies, for the rents were modest and Chase found modern conveniences very suitable to one who chronically forgot to light fires or put shillings in an electric meter. But the thinness of the walls was remarkable. Through those walls you could hear clocks strike and the pointed comments of your neighbour's wife when her husband came home late. And now it was radios, at an hour approaching midnight.

A fair-minded man, Chase tried to shut his ears against the noise. But the tenant of the ground-floor flat seemed to have a partiality for the shrillest dance bands that home or continental stations could provide, switched on at full volume. When at length he had read the same page three times without understanding a word, he decided that something would have to be done.

He got up, ran his hands through his hair with a vague idea of tidying himself, and started for the door. He was out in the corridor when the chilliness of the air reminded him that he had forgotten his coat. So he pulled on a sweater, and padded downstairs in his slippers.

Except for that radio, the whole building seemed unusually quiet. As a rule it was a shell of echoes, throwing back each gritty-sounding footstep or hum of the lift. He met nobody. Going down concrete stairs, where a faint mist had got into the bleakly lighted corridors, he turned into the passage which led to flat 10, directly below his own. And the passage was in darkness.

Trouble with the lights again, he supposed. He struck a match and groped his way down the passage. Flats 10 and 11, set side by side, occupied the end of the wing; and the music on the radio had now become a loud, confused mumble. Wondering who occupied number 10, he held the flame of the match up to the visiting-card stuck in its slot on the green-painted door. Then Douglas Chase struck another match in a hurry, and stared.

The card read: *K. G. Mills.*

Chase studied it incredulously. The thing was a coincidence, no doubt. It was impossible that this should be the formidable K. G. Mills of legend. But it gave him a start to meet the name both on duty and off, and he almost turned away from the door. But the radio decided him. He rang the bell.

"Yes, yes, yes!" called a female voice—and he was conscious of a sudden suspicion. "Just a moment, please!"

The door was dragged open. In the little green-painted entrance hall he faced a woman who could not be more than twenty-three or twenty-four, a woman with a flurried manner and ink-stained fingers. The fact that her hair was drawn back into a bun did not lessen the attractiveness of a white complexion, a full-lipped but prim-looking mouth, and a pair of extraordinarily merry blue eyes. But they were not merry now. Irresolutely she drew the back of her hand across her forehead, leaving ink-smudges there.

"Yes, yes, yes?" she inquired.

"Oh, Lord," muttered Chase. He added, on a last hope, "May I speak to Mr. Mills?"

The girl's manner changed.

"I am Mr. Mills," she said with cold dignity. "That is, I mean," she frowned and drew herself up, "to speak with academic accuracy, my name is Kathleen Gerrard Mills and I am the only Mills present at the moment. Oh, you know what I mean; but I have some terribly important research work to do, and I have been driven to such annoyance by an insufferable radio in the flat above me, that I am hardly able to say what I do mean."

Chase could hardly believe his ears.

"Madam," he said, "I am the tenant of the flat above. And I do not own a radio. In fact, I came down here to protest about yours."

Kathleen Mills's eyes, rather bemused with study, now woke up.

"But I don't own one either," she said.

She was wearing, he noticed, a grey skirt and a tight-fitting grey jumper which outlined a small, sturdy figure. She folded her arms gravely, frowned, and assumed the argumentative posture known to all dons. In one so young and attractive it might have provoked amusement if she had not been so desperately in earnest.

"This is extraordinary," she declared. "That detestable cacophony is obviously coming from somewhere. Assuming the truth of your statement, Mr.—er—"

"Chase," he said half-guiltily. "Dr. Chase. That is, University College, you know."

"Oh, my *hat!*" said the girl, shocked into naturalness.

They stood and stared at each other. Then Kathleen Mills, her colour higher, spoke with great dignity.

"How do you do?" she said formally. "While I am very pleased to make your acquaintance, Dr. Chase, I am afraid that in fairness I must take this opportunity of saying to you that I believe your views on Episcopacy in Scotland to be the merest rubbish. Indeed, as I pointed out in the *Quarterly Survey*, you hardly even appear to have heard of Nottingham's Comprehension Bill." She added, half annoyed, "And where is your beard? I thought you would have a beard."

"I must disagree with you," said Chase. "I do not refer to the beard, but to the earlier part of your remarks. And if you would do me the honour of joining me in a coffee—or beer," he added doubtfully. "You drink beer?"

"Of course I drink beer," said the girl. "And I should love to.

But I was thinking about this intolerable noise. As I say, it must come from somewhere."

It did. They heard it all about them, more muffled but very insistent. In the quiet of the big building at past midnight it had an effect that verged on the eerie. And behind Kathleen Mills's manner Chase sensed some other emotion, something far from being at ease. His eyes wandered to the dark door of number 11 beside them.

"What about the flat next door?"

"I had thought of that," she admitted, rather too quickly. "My first idea was that it came from there. But that—well, it's an empty flat: the only empty flat in the building. And it seems unlikely that anybody would be operating a radio in an empty flat."

A stir of uncertainty touched Chase: the vision of a radio playing in a dark and empty flat was what he would have called an irrational one. The girl went on speaking.

"Superstition attaching to mere dead walls and plaster is foolish. We're rational beings, Dr. Chase; at least, I hope we are. Suppose a deed of violence is done in a certain house. Well! The house is torn down to make room for another—say a block of flats. Even suppose you do believe in emanations or influences, as I do not. Is there any reason why those influences should be present in a certain one flat on the ground floor, and not in any of the flats above? It is absurd."

"Look here," Chase asked quietly. "What are you talking about?"

"Well—that flat next door. It appears that dozens of people have looked at it, and all of them have refused to take it. I'm sure I can't imagine why. There is nothing wrong with it. It's just the same as twenty others: Mr. Hemphill, the letting-agent, swears it is. But an absurd rumour has gone round that something horrible moves into it at night, and doesn't leave until morning. I told my trustee. That's Arnot Wilson, the barrister, you know; he's looked after things for me since my father died; and he was very much interested. He ridiculously tried to make jokes and frighten me about it. But after all, you know, I do sleep on the other side of the wall."

Though she smiled, the whites of her eyes had acquired an odd kind of luminousness, and she spoke with a greater rapidity. Beside the door in the angle of the wall was the tiny door of the service-hatch—dumb-waiter—to flat 11. Chase pulled it open. The inner door of the box-like hatch was also open. And now there could be no doubt.

"Yes, the radio is in there," he said. "Hear it?"

"And—and what is to be done about it?"

"Why, I'll crawl through the service-hatch and shut it off," Chase said simply.

Being long and lean, he could just manage to worm through. It was not a dignified business, stuck there with legs in the air, but he did not concern himself with that. Before he dived through the service-hatch he had accidentally touched Kathleen Mills's hand; and the hand was cold.

The entrance hall of flat 11 was dark. It smelt of mist and raw paint, and it even felt unused. He was coming closer to the core of noise, the enigmatic wireless mumbling in the dark. It appeared to be in the living-room ahead. This was an ordinary flat like his own, though he wondered what had happened to the ground where he stood. The gritty floor creaked more than it should; and the farther he moved away from the door the more he felt like a man paying out a guide-line in a cave, uncertain of his footing.

A grey window moved out at him, then a glass-panelled door. He opened the door of the living-room, meeting the noise full-blast.

An edge of a street-lamp touched two misted windows. Down in the corner by the fireplace he saw a dim shape and a tiny glowing light. For such a volume of noise it was quite a small radio, one of those convenient affairs which can be carried about by hand. It was connected to a base-plug in the wall. He switched it off; and silence descended like an extinguisher-cap.

Afterwards there was nothing. No person, no movement, no sound beyond the creak of the floor when his heel pressed it—until a fierce ringing at the outer doorbell made him jump. Until then Douglas Chase did not realize how much the hide was off his nerves, or how deep into the nerves a sudden noise could strike. He hurried to the door, turned a knob of the spring-lock, and met Kathleen.

"You seemed to be gone a long time," she told him. "Well?"

"I've turned it off," he said. "There is a radio in there, and nobody to play it or listen to it. There doesn't seem any rhyme or reason why it should be there. But there's nobody here now."

He was wrong.

It was perhaps just as well that they did not know it then. In the dim light of seven o'clock next morning, workmen constructing a boundary wall round the building passed the windows of flat number 11 on the ground floor. Through the living-room windows they saw nothing to interest them. But through the bedroom windows they saw a man huddled back into a corner as though he were trying to push himself through the wall. In appearance he was a short, stout, well-fed man, wearing an overcoat and a bowler hat. But he was dead; and they did not care to get too close to the expression on his face. James R. Hemphill, letting-agent of the flats, identified him as Mr. Arnot Wilson, barrister, of 56 Harrow Avenue, N.W.3, and the doctor in attendance said that he had died of cardiac and nervous shock caused by fright.

Two days later, when the doctor's verdict was confirmed at a post-mortem by the Home Office Analyst, certain persons gathered in a room at New Scotland Yard.

The death of Mr. Arnot Wilson had caused a minor stir. In

strictly limited circles Arnot Wilson was famous: as a "character," a persuasive lawyer, a rich after-dinner speaker, almost a public entertainer. His gentle wit had a scratch rather than a sting. He liked to collect walking-sticks and matchboxes once used by royalty. It could be said that he bounced through life. His round, guileless face; his spats and cravats; his brushed coat and glossy head; all this made a kind of india-rubber dandyism which carried him everywhere.

He lived alone, except for a cook and a man-servant, in a tall Victorian house in Harrow Avenue—not far from the block of flats where he was found dead. This house he kept too warm, with electric heaters blazing all day even in passages and in bathrooms; and almost too clean, for he was relentless to servants. Which made it all the more curious that he should be found dead of fright in an empty flat.

His body was found on Saturday morning. On Monday, Kathleen Mills and Douglas Chase were summoned to Scotland Yard. In a firelit room overlooking the Embankment they were met by a large, bland man with a speckled face, an amiable eye, and a cropped moustache. He introduced himself as Colonel March.

Colonel March's courtesy was as huge as himself.

"This," he said, "must be the dozenth time you have been troubled. But, as you understand, I must do it because my department is new to the case. I hope it does not upset you too much, Miss Mills?"

Kathleen bridled, as she always did at any hint of feminine weakness.

"I am not upset at all," she told him. "Mr. Wilson was one of my trustees. He managed the money my father left, what little there was of it. But I scarcely knew him. And—"

"You didn't like him?"

"I don't know," she replied, with an obvious struggle for honesty. "I've never been sure. All I know is that from the time I first knew him he never left off being facetious at my expense."

Suddenly she coloured, sensing an atmosphere, and broke out with violence:

"Oh, I'm being a prig and a fool! And you know it, don't you? But that's true. It was nothing but jokes, jokes, jokes; jokes about me, careers for women, our little scholar who has no boy-friends, never a pause, never a let-down in jokes. He was so tireless in it that sometimes he hardly seemed human."

Colonel March nodded gravely. Chase had not hitherto heard her speak with such frankness.

"Anyhow," she went on with a slight gesture, "there are some questions we—Dr. Chase and I—must get answered. Your people have questioned us for two days, and yet still we don't know anything. Chief Inspector—what's his name?—Chief Inspector Ames was too evasive. Will you answer four straight questions?"

"If I can," said Colonel March.

"Thank you. Well, here they are. What time did Mr. Wilson die? Did he really die of fright? Why was that radio playing? And what on earth was he doing there anyway? I happen to know he was horribly frightened of the dark."

Colonel March sat down behind a broad desk, lowering his seventeen stone with some difficulty. He looked at the desk, at the windows, at the fire, at Inspector Roberts, his second-in-command. Then he seemed to come to a decision.

"To your first two questions," he answered, clearing his throat, "I can reply. Mr. Wilson died round about eleven o'clock on Friday. And it seems that he did die of fright."

Chase could not understand the brief look of uncertainty, almost of terror, on Kathleen's face. But she spoke.

"So he was actually in the bedroom, dead, when Dr. Chase and I were in that flat?"

"He was."

"And is it—well, is it medically correct to speak of death from fright?"

"It is," said Colonel March with abrupt vehemence. "You've hit it, Miss Mills. That is why it has been given over to me, to what we call here the department of Queer Complaints. There never was a complaint queerer than this, for there are almost no precedents in law. Let's make a supposition. Let's suppose that this is murder."

It was a new and unpleasant word. Chase stirred, but Colonel March's eyes remained bland.

"I only say, let's suppose it. Suppose I find a way to frighten someone so that his heart and nervous-system are shattered as though by a blow from a gigantic hammer: that, in nontechnical language, is what the medical report means. I do not kill an invalid or a man with a weak heart, mind you. I choose a victim whose heart and nerves are sound, like Mr. Wilson. I do not touch him. But I expose to him, as though on a photographic plate, a mere sight so terrifying that his system cracks, and he dies."

Colonel March paused.

"Well, theoretically," he went on, "I am guilty of murder. That is the law. But could you get a jury to convict? I doubt it. I should say it would be impossible even to get a manslaughter verdict. Find a way to kill someone by fright, and you can commit murder almost with impunity."

Chase did not like this, because of its effect on Kathleen.

"As an interesting theory," he interposed, "it's all very well. But is there any suggestion of murder?"

"What's our alternative?" inquired Colonel March, spreading out his hands. "That the empty flat is haunted? That we are beset by ghouls and hobgoblins? That a man dare not sleep at night for literal fear of his reason or his life? I can't believe it, my friend. The only other possibility—" He stopped, breathing rather heavily. Then he went on in his normal tone. "Miss Mills, Dr. Chase, it's only fair that you should hear the evidence. Inspector, will you ask Mr. Hemphill to come in?"

They waited. James Hemphill, the letting-agent, was not slow at coming in. He was a young, affable, harassed man who seemed to regard the affair less as a death than as a further bedevilment among all the complaints. Carefully dressed, with white hands and a black line of eyebrows, he sat down gingerly in the chair Colonel March indicated.

Colonel March seemed puzzled. "Mr. Hemphill, I should like to take you over certain points in the statement you've already given to the police. Now tell me. You knew that Mr. Arnot Wilson meant to spend several hours in flat number eleven on Friday night?"

(Chase felt rather than saw Kathleen sit up.)

"Yes, I did," said Hemphill, after clearing his throat several times like a nervous orator.

"In fact, you supplied him with the key he used to get in?"

"Yes, I did."

"And you saw to it that the light in the passage was extinguished so that he would not be seen when he did go in?"

"Yes, I did."

"Why did he want to spend some hours in that flat?"

Hemphill's bristly eyebrows seemed to stand out like antennae. "Oh, it was this crazy story about number eleven being—you know, something wrong with it. He was interested. He said he'd always wanted to see a ghost."

"Had he any other reason, Mr. Hemphill?"

"Well," repeated Hemphill, after a swift, brief look at Kathleen, "he seemed to have some idea that Miss Mills was—you know, leading a double life. He thought it was very funny; he went on and on about it. He said if he listened for a few hours in the next flat on Friday night, he could catch her red-handed with her—you know, her boy-friend." Hemphill's face seemed to swell with apology. "Look here, Miss Mills, I'm dashed sorry, and it was a rotten trick; but I didn't see any actual harm in it. That's why he didn't tell you he was there."

The very face and presence of the dead man seemed to peer into the room. Arnot Wilson had often said that he was "just interested" in things.

"Oh, no. No actual harm," said Kathleen through her teeth. "It's so absolutely characteristic of him that I'm not at all surprised."

"Then there it is," explained Hemphill, with white-faced relief. "He took that radio along with him. You see, those flat-walls aren't very thick. He was afraid someone in one of the other flats might hear him walking about, and might call the police. His idea was that the noise of the radio would cover him. It's very difficult to locate the direction of sound, as you probably know; and he thought that when the other tenants heard the radio they would never connect it with an empty flat."

"He was right," observed Douglas Chase. "And if for once I might violate the rule of de mortuis, I might add that he was a damned old he-gossip who deserved what he got."

"One moment," interrupted Colonel March, whose eyes never left the letting-agent. "Admitting that he brought the radio, can you explain why he put it on with such shattering loudness that it might have roused the whole building instead of concealing his movements?"

"No, I can't explain it."

"When did you last see him alive, Mr. Hemphill?"

"About eight o'clock on Friday night. He came round and fitted up the radio in the living-room. He got rather grubby doing it, and I asked him whether he would like to wash. He said no, he would go home and wash; then he would have some sandwiches and port there, and come back about eleven. Then he left at about eight-thirty."

Colonel March walked his fingers along the edge of the desk. He seemed even more heavily disturbed.

"Eight o'clock. Yes. It was dark then; and I think there are no lights in the flat?"

"No, there aren't any lights. But I had an electric torch."

"How did Mr. Wilson relish the prospect of a vigil in the flat alone?"

After a sort of internal struggle, as though he did not know whether to grin or stammer, Hemphill blurted it out.

"I think he was as scared as blazes, if you want the truth. He tried to hide it; it was all ha-ha, my lad, and pigeon-breasted walk; but he didn't like it one little bit. I *told* him there was nothing wrong with that flat! There isn't." Then the agent's grievances came pouring out. "My company say to me, 'Why did you let him do it?' I did it to show there was nothing wrong with that flat. Who's the loser by all this? I'll tell you: I am. I shall lose my job, just notice that. But I maintain I did my duty."

"And a man died. Thank you, Mr. Hemphill; that will be all for the moment. But don't go. There is just one more witness," Colonel March added to the others, "whom you ought to hear. Inspector, will you bring in Mr. Delafield, Maurice Delafield? Delafield has been Mr. Wilson's manservant for fifteen years."

Delafield looked it, Chase decided. He was a lean, powerful, large-knuckled man whose bodily vigour contrasted with a kind of shabbiness and tiredness in his face. His greyish hair was carefully brushed and parted. A stoop took away some of his height; and, more from a late physical illness than from fear, the large-knuckled hands had a tendency to twitch and shake.

Colonel March spoke to him almost gently.

"You were with Mr. Wilson a long time, I understand?"

"Yes, sir."

"You liked him?"

"Yes, sir," said Delafield. His voice had acquired a sort of thunderous hoarseness; for one bad moment Chase was afraid he would break down and weep. But he stared steadily back at Colonel March.

"Now, we have just heard from Mr. Hemphill that Mr. Wilson left him at about eight-thirty on Friday night, with the intention of going home. Did he go home?"

"Yes, sir."

"What did he do there?"

"You see, sir, he hadn't had any dinner, he was so excited about this ghost-hunting—if you see what I mean. He had a plate of sandwiches and three glasses of port. Then he had got himself mucked up in the dirt at the empty flat, so he said he would have a bath and change his clothes. He was always very particular about that. He"—the pinkish tinge had come back to Delafield's eyelids; his voice was hoarse again—"he had his bath. Then he read the evening papers, all jumpy-like, and about ten-thirty he told me to fetch round the car. He drove away alone; and that's the last I saw of him alive."

"Tell me: you laid out the suit of clothes he wore that night?"

"Yes, sir. I laid it out."

Selecting a paper from a pile on his desk, the colonel handed it across.

"Here we are. Here's a list of all the things found in Mr. Wilson's pockets when the body was discovered: or in the flat itself, for that matter. 'Address-book. Fountain-pen. Key-ring, six keys. Separate key to flat number eleven. Watch and chain. Notecase with eight pounds in notes. Ten and ninepence in silver and coppers.' Will you check this over carefully and tell me whether it is everything he took with him?"

Though Delafield tried hard, his dry fingers rustled and shook on the paper. It slipped through his fingers, and he gave it a curious despairing look, like an angler who has lost a fish.

He said desperately:

"I'm very sorry, sir. I'm not scared. Honestly, I'm not. But I haven't been well. Mr. Wilson wouldn't even let me shave him recently; he would say, over and over, over and over, 'You will be cutting my throat one of these days; and then they will hang you, because I have remembered you in my will.' "

Delafield sat down again, after picking up the paper, holding it in two hands, and putting it on Colonel March's desk. He continued to talk in the same vein until Kathleen cut him short gently.

"Does anybody doubt, please," she said, "the sort of man my esteemed Mr. Arnot Wilson really was? Or, as Dr. Chase says, whether he deserved what he got?"

"That's not true, miss! It's not!"

"True or not, it is hardly our point," interrupted Colonel March, in a tone he very seldom used. They all looked at him; his sandy eyebrows were drawn down, and his eyes were as fixed as though he were trying to draw the witness under hypnosis. "I have asked you a question, Mr. Delafield. Is that list correct?"

"Yes, sir."

"You're positive he took nothing else?"

"Positive, sir."

"I see. Then I am glad to inform you," observed Colonel March, "that this is not a supernatural crime nor a supernatural death."

There was a change in the atmosphere as palpable as a chilling or darkening of the room. Colonel March alone seemed unaffected by it. On the contrary, the blood had come back into his face and he was tuned up to a ferocious geniality. For the first time he picked up a fat-bowled pipe from his desk.

"It was murder," he went on, rapping the pipe on the edge of an ashtray. "The victim did not die of fright. He died from a cause commoner and better known. I said a while ago that there was another possibility. It remains to be seen whether I can prove this. We discarded the other possibility after the post-mortem, because circumstances seemed to rule it out. And yet there is just one other way in which a man can be killed with no other symptoms, external or internal, than that terrific hammer-blow to the heart and nervous system."

Hemphill spoke in a high voice. "If there aren't any symptoms, I don't see how you can prove it, though I hope to heaven you can. But how would you kill a man like that?"

"By passing a current of electricity through his bath-water," said Colonel March. He turned to Delafield. "Would you care to tell us how you killed him, or shall I?"

Inspector Roberts rose to his feet at the other side of the room, but it was not necessary. Delafield sat with his large-knuckled hands pressed together, nodding. Otherwise he did not move: but it was as though the shabbiness of his face increased.

"I'll tell you," he said simply. "If only you'll honest-to-God believe it was an accident."

"One moment," urged Colonel March. He hesitated; and his forehead was clouded. "I want you to understand that you are not obliged to answer—"

"Oh, that's all right," said Delafield, making an off-handed gesture. "I want these gentlemen and this lady to bear me out. I didn't mean to tell you unless you guessed it. But *I* didn't mean him any harm."

With the same air of toiling lucidity he unclasped his hands and held them up.

"These did it," he explained. "Maybe you know, sir, how warm Mr. Wilson liked to have the house? And how he had portable electric fires going everywhere all day, even in the passages and in the bathrooms?"

"Yes," said Colonel March quietly.

Delafield nodded. "I dropped one of the electric heaters into the bath," he said. "That's all. That's how bad and simple it all was. Mr. Wilson told me I might do it. Over and over he kept telling me how I might do it, not meaning to. It was a kind of nightmare with me, thinking I might do it with these hands; and then he joggled my arm—

"You see, sir, Mr. Wilson read in the paper long ago how several people had got killed like that. At Bristol, I think it was. Accidents. It was a cold day, and they had propped them fires up on ledges by the bath. You wouldn't think people would be foolish enough to do that, but that's what they did. Mr. Wilson didn't do that, of course. But he liked lots of heat, and he liked to have the fire standing close to the bath.

"He was frightened of things like that. Over and over he said to me, 'Don't you do that to me, or they'll hang you for murder.' Like the shaving, you see, sir. It got so I couldn't look at an electric fire in the bathroom without being nervous. And he read up on the symptoms of being electrocuted like that, in a book called *Taylor's Medical Jurisprudence*, I think it was; him being a lawyer and all; and he was surprised at what the symptoms were.

"I expect I was off-guard on Friday night, with him talking so much about ghosts. He got into the bath. Then without thinking he called to me to move the heater closer to the bath. I picked it up in my hand, not thinking either. All of a sudden he shouted out to me, and said, 'Put it down, you damned doddering old fool!' and made a grab for my hand."

Again Delafield examined his hands. It was very quiet in the room. Kathleen had got up and put her own hand on his shoulder.

"It fell," he added.

"Afterwards I was afraid they would hang me, just like Mr. Wilson said, if they knew how it happened. I thought if I could pretend it happened some other way they wouldn't find out. It said in the book that the symptoms for this kind of electrocution were the same as the symptoms of death from fright; and poor Mr. Wilson had always been frightened of ghosts and the dark.

"So I moved him. First I dressed him: which wasn't hard, because that's what I've been doing for years. I carried him down-stairs. That wasn't hard either, because I'm a pretty hefty specimen, as you can see; and he wasn't what you could call big. The car was at the door. I wasn't much afraid of being seen moving him, because the night was so misty.

"I had his key to the flat, and I knew what he was going to do. I knew the light would be out in the hall leading to the flat; and the service-door was near that. I put him down in the bedroom of the flat about eleven o'clock. Then I turned on the wireless and left. I put it on loud and strong so that somebody *should* find him soon; I didn't want him lying there all that time alone.

"That's all. Maybe he was difficult, but I've served him for fifteen years, and you sort of get used to people. He didn't die hard; just a kind of a cry, and he fell back. All the same, I can't forget it, so I've been wanting to tell you. I suppose they'll hang me, but I swear I didn't mean any harm."

Kathleen tightened her grip on his shoulder. Chase, drawn by currents of sympathy as strong as electric currents, faced Colonel March.

"Sir," Chase said, "they surely won't—"

Colonel March shook his head. He studied Delafield with a long, thoughtful look.

"If he is telling the truth," said the head of Department D-3, "they assuredly won't. I question whether anything will be done to him at all. And somehow I suspect he is telling the truth. I shall turn in my report to that effect."

Kathleen blinked a little, and the more so when Chase's fingers closed round her hand.

"May I—er—apologize for what I was thinking of you?" she said to Colonel March. "Perhaps Arnot Wilson was right after all; perhaps I do think I know too much. But will you kindly, kindly enlighten a scientific curiosity on just one point? How on earth did you know what had happened?"

"Oh, that?" grunted Colonel March, blinking and suddenly chuckling at the vehemence with which she assailed him. "That wasn't difficult. The Queer Complaints department had much more trouble with a doorbell-ringer at Hammersmith. It certainly wasn't difficult once you had grasped the crucial fact that Wilson had not died in the flat: he had been conveyed there after death.

"It seemed almost certain he had not walked there in life, because he had failed to take something he would never have gone there without. We did not find it either in his pockets or anywhere else in the flat. Everybody commented on Arnot Wilson's morbid fear of the dark. I could believe he might screw up enough courage to go there, particularly since he had the added incentive of spying on you. But I could not believe he would face the prospect of several hours alone in a supposedly haunted flat without taking along either an electric torch, a candle, or even a box of matches."

DR. FELL STORIES

The Incautious Burglar

Two guests, who were not staying the night at Cranleigh Court, left at shortly past eleven o'clock. Marcus Hunt saw them to the front door. Then he returned to the dining-room, where the poker-chips were now stacked into neat piles of white, red, and blue.

"Another game?" suggested Rolfe.

"No good," said Derek Henderson. His tone, as usual, was weary. "Not with just the three of us."

Their host stood by the sideboard and watched them. The long, low house, overlooking the Weald of Kent, was so quiet that their voices rose with startling loudness. The dining-room, large and panelled, was softly lighted by electric wall-candles which brought out the sombre colours of the paintings. It is not often that anybody sees, in one room of an otherwise commonplace country house, two Rembrandts and a Van Dyck. There was a kind of defiance about those paintings.

To Arthur Rolfe—the art dealer—they represented enough money to make him shiver. To Derek Henderson—the art critic—they represented a problem. What they represented to Marcus Hunt was not apparent.

Hunt stood by the sideboard, his fists on his hips, smiling. He was a middle-sized, stocky man, with a full face and a high complexion. Equip him with a tuft of chin-whisker, and he would have looked like a Dutch burgher for a Dutch brush. His shirt-front bulged out untidily. He watched with ironical amusement

41

while Henderson picked up a pack of cards in long fingers, cut them into two piles, and shuffled with a sharp flick of each thumb which made the cards melt together like a conjuring trick.

Henderson yawned.

"My boy," said Hunt, "you surprise me."

"That's what I try to do," answered Henderson, still wearily. He looked up. "But why do you say so, particularly?"

Henderson was young, he was long, he was lean, he was immaculate; and he wore a beard. It was a reddish beard, which moved some people to hilarity. But he wore it with an air of complete naturalness.

"I'm surprised," said Hunt, "that you enjoy anything so bourgeois—so plebeian—as poker."

"I enjoy reading people's characters," said Henderson. "Poker's the best way to do it, you know."

Hunt's eyes narrowed. "Oh? Can you read my character, for instance?"

"With pleasure," said Henderson. Absently he dealt himself a poker-hand, face up. It contained a pair of fives, and the last card was the ace of spades. Henderson remained staring at it for a few seconds before he glanced up again.

"And I can tell you," he went on, "that you surprise me. Do you mind if I'm frank? I had always thought of you as the Colossus of Business; the smasher; the plunger; the fellow who took the long chances. Now, you're not like that at all."

Marcus Hunt laughed. But Henderson was undisturbed.

"You're tricky, but you're cautious. I doubt if you ever took a long chance in your life. Another surprise"—he dealt himself a new hand—"is Mr. Rolfe here. He's the man who, given the proper circumstances, would take the long chances."

Arthur Rolfe considered this. He looked startled, but rather flattered. Though in height and build not unlike Hunt, there was nothing untidy about him. He had a square, dark face, with thin shells of eyeglasses, and a worried forehead.

"I doubt that," he declared, very serious about this. Then he smiled. "A person who took long chances in my business would find himself in the soup." He glanced round the room. "Anyhow, I'd be too cautious to have three pictures, with an aggregate value of thirty thousand pounds, hanging in an unprotected downstairs room with French windows giving on a terrace." An almost frenzied note came into his voice. "Great Scot! Suppose a burglar—"

"Damn!" said Henderson unexpectedly.

Even Hunt jumped.

Ever since the poker-party, an uneasy atmosphere had been growing. Hunt had picked up an apple from a silver fruit-bowl on the sideboard. He was beginning to pare it with a fruit-knife, a sharp wafer-thin blade which glittered in the light of the wall-lamps.

"You nearly made me slice my thumb off," he said, putting down the knife. "What's the matter with you?"

"It's the ace of spades," said Henderson, still languidly. "That's the second time it's turned up in five minutes."

Arthur Rolfe chose to be dense. "Well? What about it?"

"I think our young friend is being psychic," said Hunt, good-humoured again. "Are you reading characters, or only telling fortunes?"

Henderson hesitated. His eyes moved to Hunt, and then to the wall over the sideboard where Rembrandt's "Old Woman with Cap" stared back with the immobility and skin-colouring of a red Indian. Then Henderson looked towards the French windows opening on the terrace.

"None of my affair," shrugged Henderson. "It's your house and your collection and your responsibility. But this fellow Butler: what do you know about him?"

Marcus Hunt looked boisterously amused.

"Butler? He's a friend of my niece's. Harriet picked him up in London, and asked me to invite him down here. Nonsense! Butler's all right. What are you thinking, exactly?"

"Listen!" said Rolfe, holding up his hand.

The noise they heard, from the direction of the terrace, was not repeated. It was not repeated because the person who had made it, a very bewildered and uneasy young lady, had run lightly and swiftly to the far end, where she leaned against the balustrade.

Lewis Butler hesitated before going after her. The moonlight was so clear that one could see the mortar between the tiles which paved the terrace, and trace the design of the stone urns along the balustrade. Harriet Davis wore a white gown with long and filmy skirts, which she lifted clear of the ground as she ran.

Then she beckoned to him.

She was half sitting, half leaning against the rail. Her white arms were spread out, fingers gripping the stone. Dark hair and dark eyes became even more vivid by moonlight. He could see the rapid rise and fall of her breast; he could even trace the shadow of her eyelashes.

"That was a lie, anyhow," she said.

"What was?"

"What my uncle Marcus said. You heard him." Harriet Davis's fingers tightened still more on the balustrade. But she nodded her head vehemently, with fierce accusation. "About my knowing you. And inviting you here. I never saw you before this weekend. Either Uncle Marcus is going out of his mind, or . . . will you answer me just one question?"

"If I can."

"Very well. Are you by any chance a crook?"

She spoke with as much simplicity and directness as though she had asked him whether he might be a doctor or a lawyer. Lewis

Butler was not unwise enough to laugh. She was in that mood where, to any woman, laughter is salt to a raw wound; she would probably have slapped his face.

"To be quite frank about it," he said, "I'm not. Will you tell me why you asked?"

"This house," said Harriet, looking at the moon, "used to be guarded with burglar alarms. If you as much as touched a window, the whole place started clanging like a fire-station. He had all the burglar alarms removed last week. Last week." She took her hands off the balustrade, and pressed them together hard. "The pictures used to be upstairs, in a locked room next to his bedroom. He had them moved downstairs—last week. It's almost as though my uncle wanted the house to be burgled."

Butler knew that he must use great care here.

"Perhaps he does." (Here she looked at Butler quickly, but did not comment.) "For instance," he went on idly, "suppose one of his famous Rembrandts turned out to be a fake? It might be a relief not to have to show it to his expert friends."

The girl shook her head.

"No," she said. "They're all genuine. You see, I thought of that too."

Now was the time to hit, and hit hard. To Lewis Butler, in his innocence, there seemed to be no particular problem. He took out his cigarette-case, and turned it over without opening it.

"Look here, Miss Davis, you're not going to like this. But I can tell you of cases in which people were rather anxious to have their property 'stolen.' If a picture is insured for more than its value, and then it is mysteriously 'stolen' one night—?"

"That might be all very well too," answered Harriet, still calmly. "Except that not one of those pictures has been insured."

The cigarette-case, which was of polished metal, slipped through Butler's fingers and fell with a clatter on the tiles. It spilled cigarettes, just as it spilled and confused his theories. As he bent over to pick it up, he could hear a church clock across the Weald strike the half-hour after eleven.

"You're sure of that?"

"I'm perfectly sure. He hasn't insured any of his pictures for as much as a penny. He says it's a waste of money."

"But—"

"Oh, I know! And I don't know why I'm talking to you like this. You're a stranger, aren't you?" She folded her arms, drawing her shoulders up as though she were cold. Uncertainty, fear, and plain nerves flicked at her eyelids. "But then Uncle Marcus is a stranger too. Do you know what I think? *I* think he's going mad."

"Hardly as bad as that, is it?"

"Yes, go on," the girl suddenly stormed at him. "Say it: go on and say it. That's easy enough. But you don't see him when his eyes seem to get smaller, and all that genial-country-squire look goes out of his face. He's not a fake: he hates fakes, and goes out of his way to expose them. But, if he hasn't gone clear out of his mind, what's he up to? What can he be up to?"

In something over three hours they found out.

The burglar did not attack until half-past two in the morning. First he smoked several cigarettes in the shrubbery below the rear terrace. When he heard the church clock strike, he waited a few minutes more, and then slipped up the steps to the French windows of the dining-room.

A chilly wind stirred at the turn of the night, in the hour of suicides and bad dreams. It smoothed grass and trees with a faint rustling. When the man glanced over his shoulder, the last of the moonlight distorted his face: it showed less a face than the blob of a black cloth mask under a greasy cap pulled down over his ears.

He went to work on the middle window, with the contents of a folding tool-kit not so large as a motorist's. He fastened two short strips of adhesive tape to the glass just beside the catch. Then his glass-cutter sliced out a small semi-circle inside the tape.

It was done not without noise: it crunched like a dentist's drill in a tooth, and the man stopped to listen.

There was no answering noise. No dog barked.

With the adhesive tape holding the glass so that it did not fall and smash, he slid his gloved hand through the opening and twisted the catch. The weight of his body deadened the creaking of the window when he pushed inside.

He knew exactly what he wanted. He put the tool-kit into his pocket, and drew out an electric torch. Its beam moved across to the sideboard; it touched gleaming silver, a bowl of fruit, and a wicked little knife thrust into an apple as though into someone's body; finally, it moved up the hag-face of the "Old Woman with Cap."

This was not a large picture, and the burglar lifted it down easily. He pried out glass and frame. Though he tried to roll up the canvas with great care, the brittle paint cracked across in small stars which wounded the hag's face. The burglar was so intent on this that he never noticed the presence of another person in the room.

He was an incautious burglar: he had no sixth sense which smelt murder.

Up on the second floor of the house, Lewis Butler was awakened by a muffled crash like that of metal objects falling.

He had not fallen into more than a half doze all night. He knew with certainty what must be happening, though he had no idea of why, or how, or to whom.

Butler was out of bed, and into his slippers, as soon as he heard the first faint clatter from downstairs. His dressing-gown would, as usual, twist itself up like a rolled umbrella and defy all attempts to find the arm-holes whenever he wanted to hurry. But the little flashlight was ready in the pocket.

That noise seemed to have roused nobody else. With certain

possibilities in his mind, he had never in his life moved so fast once he managed to get out of his bedroom. Not using his light, he was down two flights of deep-carpeted stairs without noise. In the lower hall he could feel a draught, which meant that a window or door had been opened somewhere. He made straight for the dining-room.

But he was too late.

Once the pencil-beam of Butler's flashlight had swept round, he switched on a whole blaze of lights. The burglar was still here, right enough. But the burglar was lying very still in front of the sideboard; and, to judge by the amount of blood on his sweater and trousers, he would never move again.

"That's done it," Butler said aloud.

A silver service, including a tea-urn, had been toppled off the sideboard. Where the fruit-bowl had fallen, the dead man lay on his back among a litter of oranges, apples, and a squashed bunch of grapes. The mask still covered the burglar's face; his greasy cap was flattened still further on his ears; his gloved hands were thrown wide.

Fragments of smashed picture-glass lay round him, together with the empty frame, and the "Old Woman with Cap" had been half crumpled up under his body. From the position of the most conspicuous bloodstains, one judged that he had been stabbed through the chest with the stained fruit-knife beside him.

"What is it?" said a voice almost at Butler's ear.

He could not have been more startled if the fruit-knife had pricked his ribs. He had seen nobody turning on lights in the hall, nor had he heard Harriet Davis approach. She was standing just behind him, wrapped in a Japanese kimono, with her dark hair round her shoulders. But, when he explained what had happened, she would not look into the dining-room; she backed away, shaking her head violently, like an urchin ready for flight.

"You had better wake up your uncle," Butler said briskly, with

a confidence he did not feel. "And the servants. I must use your
telephone." Then he looked her in the eyes. "Yes, you're quite
right. I think you've guessed it already. I'm a police-officer."

She nodded.

"Yes. I guessed. Who are you? And is your name really Butler?"

"I'm a sergeant of the Criminal Investigation Department. And
my name really is Butler. Your uncle brought me here."

"Why?"

"I don't know. He hasn't got round to telling me."

This girl's intelligence, even when over-shadowed by fear, was
direct and disconcerting. "But, if he wouldn't say why he wanted
a police-officer, how did they come to send you? He'd have to tell
them, wouldn't he?"

Butler ignored it. "I must see your uncle. Will you go upstairs
and wake him, please?"

"I can't," said Harriet. "Uncle Marcus isn't in his room."

"Isn't—?"

"No. I knocked at the door on my way down. He's gone."

Butler took the stairs two treads at a time. Harriet had turned
on all the lights on her way down, but nothing stirred in the bleak,
over-decorated passages.

Marcus Hunt's bedroom was empty. His dinner-jacket had been
hung up neatly on the back of a chair, shirt laid across the seat
with collar and tie on top of it. Hunt's watch ticked loudly on the
dressing-table. His money and keys were there too. But he had not
gone to bed, for the bedspread was undisturbed.

The suspicion which came to Lewis Butler, listening to the thin
insistent ticking of that watch in the drugged hour before dawn,
was so fantastic that he could not credit it.

He started downstairs again, and on the way he met Arthur
Rolfe blundering out of another bedroom down the hall. The art
dealer's stocky body was wrapped in a flannel dressing-gown. He
was not wearing his eyeglasses, which gave his face a bleary and

rather caved-in expression. He planted himself in front of Butler, and refused to budge.

"Yes," said Butler. "You don't have to ask. It's a burglar."

"I knew it," said Rolfe calmly. "Did he get anything?"

"No. He was murdered."

For a moment Rolfe said nothing, but his hand crept into the breast of his dressing-gown as though he felt pain there.

"Murdered? You don't mean the burglar was murdered?"

"Yes."

"But why? By an accomplice, you mean? Who is the burglar?"

"That," snarled Lewis Butler, "is what I intend to find out."

In the lower hall he found Harriet Davis, who was now standing in the doorway of the dining-room and looking steadily at the body by the sideboard. Though her face hardly moved a muscle, her eyes brimmed over.

"You're going to take off the mask, aren't you?" she asked, without turning round.

Stepping with care to avoid squashed fruit and broken glass, Butler leaned over the dead man. He pushed back the peak of the greasy cap; he lifted the black cloth mask, which was clumsily held by an elastic band; and he found what he expected to find.

The burglar was Marcus Hunt—stabbed through the heart while attempting to rob his own house.

"You see, sir," Butler explained to Dr. Gideon Fell on the following afternoon, "that's the trouble. However you look at it, the case makes no sense."

Again he went over the facts.

"Why should the man burgle his own house and steal his own property? Every one of those paintings is valuable, and not a single one is insured! Consequently, why? Was the man a simple lunatic? What did he think he was doing?"

The village of Sutton Valence, straggling like a grey-white Italian town along the very peak of the Weald, was full of hot sunshine. In the apple orchard behind the white inn of the *Tabard*, Dr. Gideon Fell sat at a garden table among wasps, with a pint tankard at his elbow. Dr. Fell's vast bulk was clad in a white linen suit. His pink face smoked in the heat, and his wary lookout for wasps gave him a regrettably wall-eyed appearance as he pondered.

He said:

"Superintendent Hadley suggested that I might—harrumph— look in here. The local police are in charge, aren't they?"

"Yes. I'm merely standing by."

"Hadley's exact words to me were, 'It's so crazy that nobody but you will understand it.' The man's flattery becomes more nauseating every day." Dr. Fell scowled. "I say. Does anything else strike you as queer about this business?"

"Well, why should a man burgle his own house?"

"No, no, no!" growled Dr. Fell. "Don't be obsessed with that point. Don't become hypnotized by it. For instance"—a wasp hovered near his tankard, and he distended his cheeks and blew it away with one vast puff like Father Neptune—"for instance, the young lady seems to have raised an interesting question. If Marcus Hunt wouldn't say why he wanted a detective in the house, why did the C.I.D. consent to send you?"

Butler shrugged his shoulders.

"Because," he said, "Chief Inspector Ames thought Hunt was up to funny business, and meant to stop it."

"What sort of funny business?"

"A faked burglary to steal his own pictures for the insurance. It looked like the old, old game of appealing to the police to divert suspicion. In other words, sir, exactly what this appeared to be: until I learned (and to-day proved) that not one of those damned pictures has ever been insured for a penny."

Butler hesitated.

"It can't have been a practical joke," he went on. "Look at the elaborateness of it! Hunt put on old clothes from which all tailors' tabs and laundry marks were removed. He put on gloves and a mask. He got hold of a torch and an up-to-date kit of burglar's tools. He went out of the house by the back door; we found it open later. He smoked a few cigarettes in the shrubbery below the terrace; we found his footprints in the soft earth. He cut a pane of glass . . . but I've told you all that."

"And then," mused Dr. Fell, "somebody killed him."

"Yes. The last and worst 'why.' Why should anybody have killed him?"

"H'm. Clues?"

"Negative." Butler took out his notebook. "According to the police surgeon, he died of a direct heart-wound from a blade (presumably that fruit-knife) so thin that the wound was difficult to find. There were a number of his fingerprints, but nobody else's. We did find one odd thing, though. A number of pieces in the silver service off the sideboard were scratched in a queer way. It looked almost as though, instead of being swept off the sideboard in a struggle, they had been piled up on top of each other like a tower; and then pushed—"

Butler paused, for Dr. Fell was shaking his big head back and forth with an expression of Gargantuan distress.

"Well, well, well," he was saying; "well, well, well. And you call that negative evidence?"

"Isn't it? It doesn't explain why a man burgles his own house."

"Look here," said the doctor mildly. "I should like to ask you just one question. What is the most important point in this affair? One moment! I did not say the most interesting; I said the most important. Surely it is the fact that a man has been murdered?"

"Yes, sir. Naturally."

"I mention the fact"—the doctor was apologetic—"because it seems in danger of being overlooked. It hardly interests you. You are concerned only with Hunt's senseless masquerade. You don't mind a throat being cut; but you can't stand a leg being pulled. Why not try working at it from the other side, and asking who killed Hunt?"

Butler was silent for a long time.

"The servants are out of it," he said at length. "They sleep in another wing on the top floor; and for some reason," he hesitated, "somebody locked them in last night." His doubts, even his dreads, were beginning to take form. "There was a fine blow-up over that when the house was roused. Of course, the murderer could have been an outsider."

"You know it wasn't," said Dr. Fell. "Would you mind taking me to Cranleigh Court?"

They came out on the terrace in the hottest part of the afternoon.

Dr. Fell sat down on a wicker settee, with a dispirited Harriet beside him. Derek Henderson, in flannels, perched his long figure on the balustrade. Arthur Rolfe alone wore a dark suit and seemed out of place. For the pale green and brown of the Kentish lands, which rarely acquired harsh colour, now blazed. No air stirred, no leaf moved, in that brilliant thickness of heat; and down in the garden, towards their left, the water of the swimming-pool sparkled with hot, hard light. Butler felt it like a weight on his eyelids.

Derek Henderson's beard was at once languid and yet aggressive.

"It's no good," he said. "Don't keep on asking me why Hunt should have burgled his own house. But I'll give you a tip."

"Which is?" inquired Dr. Fell.

"Whatever the reason was," returned Henderson, sticking out his neck, "it was a good reason. Hunt was much too canny and cautious ever to do anything without a good reason. I told him so last night."

Dr. Fell spoke sharply. "Cautious? Why do you say that?"

"Well, for instance. I take three cards on the draw. Hunt takes one. I bet; he sees me and raises. I cover that, and raise again. Hunt drops out. In other words, it's fairly certain he's filled his hand, but not so certain I'm holding much more than a pair. Yet Hunt drops out. So with my three sevens I bluff him out of his straight. He played a dozen hands last night just like that."

Henderson began to chuckle. Seeing the expression on Harriet's face, he checked himself and became preternaturally solemn.

"But then, of course," Henderson added, "he had a lot on his mind last night."

Nobody could fail to notice the change of tone.

"So? And what did he have on his mind?"

"Exposing somebody he had always trusted," replied Henderson coolly. "That's why I didn't like it when the ace of spades turned up so often."

"You'd better explain that," said Harriet, after a pause. "I don't know what you're hinting at, but you'd better explain that. He told you he intended to expose somebody he had always trusted?"

"No. Like myself, he hinted at it."

It was the stolid Rolfe who stormed into the conversation then. Rolfe had the air of a man determined to hold hard to reason, but finding it difficult.

"Listen to me," snapped Rolfe. "I have heard a great deal, at one time or another, about Mr. Hunt's liking for exposing people. Very well!" He slid one hand into the breast of his coat, in a characteristic gesture. "But where in the name of sanity does that leave us? He wants to expose someone. And, to do that, he puts on outlandish clothes and masquerades as a burglar. Is that sensible? I tell you, the man was mad! There's no other explanation."

"There are five other explanations," said Dr. Fell.

Derek Henderson slowly got up from his seat on the balustrade, but he sat down again at a savage gesture from Rolfe.

Nobody spoke.

"I will not, however," pursued Dr. Fell, "waste your time with four of them. We are concerned with only one explanation: the real one."

"And you know the real one?" asked Henderson sharply.

"I rather think so."

"Since when?"

"Since I had the opportunity of looking at all of you," answered Dr. Fell.

He settled back massively in the wicker settee, so that its frame creaked and cracked like a ship's bulkhead in a heavy sea. His vast chin was outthrust, and he nodded absently as though to emphasize some point that was quite clear in his own mind.

"I've already had a word with the local inspector," he went on suddenly. "He will be here in a few minutes. And, at my suggestion, he will have a request for all of you. I sincerely hope nobody will refuse."

"Request?" said Henderson. "What request?"

"It's a very hot day," said Dr. Fell, blinking towards the swimming-pool. "He's going to suggest that you all go in for a swim."

Harriet uttered a kind of despairing mutter, and turned as though appealing to Lewis Butler.

"That," continued Dr. Fell, "will be the politest way of drawing attention to the murderer. In the meantime, let me call your attention to one point in the evidence which seems to have been generally overlooked. Mr. Henderson, do you know anything about direct heart-wounds, made by a steel blade as thin as a wafer?"

"Like Hunt's wound? No. What about them?"

"There is practically no exterior bleeding," answered Dr. Fell.

"But—!" Harriet was beginning, when Butler stopped her.

"The police surgeon, in fact, called attention to that wound which was so 'difficult to find.' The victim dies almost at once; and the edges of the wound compress. But in that case," argued Dr. Fell, "how did the late Mr. Hunt come to have so much blood on his sweater, and even splashed on his trousers?"

"Well?"

"He didn't," answered Dr. Fell simply. "Mr. Hunt's blood never got on his clothes at all."

"I can't stand this," said Harriet, jumping to her feet. "I—I'm sorry, but have you gone mad yourself? Are you telling us we didn't see him lying by that sideboard, with blood on him?"

"Oh, yes. You saw that."

"Let him go on," said Henderson, who was rather white round the nostrils. "Let him rave."

"It is, I admit, a fine point," said Dr. Fell. "But it answers your question, repeated to the point of nausea, as to why the eminently sensible Mr. Hunt chose to dress up in burglar's clothes and play burglar. The answer is short and simple. He didn't."

"It must be plain to everybody," Dr. Fell went on, opening his eyes wide, "that Mr. Hunt was deliberately setting a trap for some-one—the real burglar.

"He believed that a certain person might try to steal one or several of his pictures. He probably knew that this person had tried similar games before, in other country houses: that is, an inside job which was carefully planned to look like an outside job. So he made things easy for this thief, in order to trap him, with a police-officer in the house.

"The burglar, a sad fool, fell for it. This thief, a guest in the house, waited until well past two o'clock in the morning. He then put on his old clothes, mask, gloves, and the rest of it. He let him-self out by the back door. He went through all the motions we have erroneously been attributing to Marcus Hunt. Then the trap snapped. Just as he was rolling up the Rembrandt, he heard a noise. He swung his light round. And he saw Marcus Hunt, in pyjamas and dressing-gown, looking at him.

"Yes, there was a fight. Hunt flew at him. The thief snatched up a fruit-knife and fought back. In that struggle, Marcus Hunt forced his opponent's hand back. The fruit-knife gashed the thief's chest, inflicting a superficial but badly bleeding gash. It sent the thief over the edge of insanity. He wrenched Marcus Hunt's wrist half off, caught up the knife, and stabbed Hunt to the heart.

"Then, in a quiet house, with a little beam of light streaming out from the torch on the sideboard, the murderer sees something that will hang him. He sees the blood from his own superficial wound seeping down his clothes.

"How is he to get rid of those clothes? He cannot destroy them, or get them away from the house. Inevitably the house will be searched, and they will be found. Without the blood-stains, they would seem ordinary clothes in his wardrobe. But with the blood-stains—"

"There is only one thing he can do."

Harriet Davis was standing behind the wicker settee, shading her eyes against the glare of the sun. Her hand did not tremble when she said:

"He changed clothes with my uncle."

"That's it," growled Dr. Fell. "That's the whole sad story. The murderer dressed the body in his own clothes, making a puncture with the knife in sweater, shirt, and undervest. He then slipped on Mr. Hunt's pyjamas and dressing-gown, which at a pinch he could always claim as his own. Hunt's wound had bled hardly at all. His dressing-gown, I think, had come open in the fight, so that all the thief had to trouble him was a tiny puncture in the jacket of the pyjamas.

"But, once he had done this, he had to hypnotize you all into the belief that there would have been no time for a change of clothes. He had to make it seem that the fight occurred just *then*. He had to rouse the house. So he brought down echoing thunders by pushing over a pile of silver, and slipped upstairs."

Dr. Fell paused.

"The burglar could never have been Marcus Hunt, you know,"

he added. "We learn that Hunt's fingerprints were all over the place. Yet the murdered man was wearing gloves."

There was a swishing of feet in the grass below the terrace, and a tread of heavy boots coming up the terrace steps. The local Inspector of police, buttoned up and steaming in his uniform, was followed by two constables.

Dr. Fell turned round a face of satisfaction.

"Ah!" he said, breathing deeply. "They've come to see about that swimming-party, I imagine. It is easy to patch up a flesh-wound with lint and cotton, or even a handkerchief. But such a wound will become infernally conspicuous in anyone who is forced to climb into bathing-trunks."

"But it couldn't have been—" cried Harriet. Her eyes moved round. Her fingers tightened on Lewis Butler's arm, an instinctive gesture which he was to remember long afterwards, when he knew her even better.

"Exactly," agreed the doctor, wheezing with pleasure. "It could not have been a long, thin, gangling fellow like Mr. Henderson. It assuredly could not have been a small and slender girl like yourself.

"There is only one person who, as we know, is just about Marcus Hunt's height and build; who could have put his own clothes on Hunt without any suspicion. That is the same person who, though he managed to staunch the wound in his chest, has been constantly running his hand inside the breast of his coat to make certain the bandage is secure. Just as Mr. Rolfe is doing now."

Arthur Rolfe sat very quiet, with his right hand still in the breast of his jacket. His face had grown smeary in the hot sunlight, but the eyes behind those thin shells of glasses remained inscrutable. He spoke only once, through dry lips, after they had cautioned him.

"I should have taken the young pup's warning," he said. "After all, he told me I would take long chances."

Invisible Hands

He could never understand afterward why he felt uneasiness, even to the point of fear, before he saw the beach at all.

Night and fancies? But how far can fancies go?

It was a steep track down to the beach. The road, however, was good, and he could rely on his car. And yet, halfway down, before he could even taste the sea-wind or hear the rustle of the sea, Dan Fraser felt sweat on his forehead. A nerve jerked in the calf of his leg over the foot brake.

"Look, this is damn silly!" he thought to himself. He thought it with a kind of surprise, as when he had first known fear in war-time long ago. But the fear had been real enough, no matter how well he concealed it, and they believed he never felt it.

A dazzle of lightning lifted ahead of him. The night was too hot. This enclosed road, bumping the springs of his car, seemed pressed down in an airless hollow.

After all, Dan Fraser decided, he had everything to be thankful for. He was going to see Brenda; he was the luckiest man in London. If she chose to spend weekends as far away as North Cornwall, he was glad to drag himself there—even a day late.

Brenda's image rose before him, as clearly as the flash of lightning. He always seemed to see her half laughing, half pouting, with light on her yellow hair. She was beautiful; she was desirable. It would only be disloyalty to think any trickiness underlay her intense, naïve ways.

Brenda Lestrange always got what she wanted. And she had

wanted him, though God alone knew why: he was no prize package at all. Again, in imagination, he saw her against the beat and shuffle of music in a night club. Brenda's shoulders rose from a low-cut silver gown, her eyes as blue and wide-spaced as the eternal Eve's.

You'd have thought she would have preferred a dasher, a roaring bloke like Toby Curtis, who had all the women after him. But that, as Joyce had intimated, might be the trouble. Toby Curtis couldn't see Brenda for all the rest of the crowd. And so Brenda preferred—

Well, then, what was the matter with him?

He would see Brenda in a few minutes. There ought to have been joy bells in the tower, not bats in the—

Easy!

He was out in the open now, at sea level. Dan Fraser drove bumpingly along scrub grass, at the head of a few shallow terraces leading down to the private beach. Ahead of him, facing seaward, stood the overlarge, overdecorated bungalow which Brenda had rather grandly named "The King's House."

And there wasn't a light in it—not a light showing at only a quarter past ten.

Dan cut the engine, switched off the lights, and got out of the car. In the darkness he could hear the sea charge the beach as an army might have charged it.

Twisting open the handle of the car's trunk, he dragged out his suitcase. He closed the compartment with a slam which echoed out above the swirl of water. This part of the Cornish coast was too lonely, too desolate, but it was the first time such a thought had ever occurred to him.

He went to the house, round the side and toward the front. His footsteps clacked loudly on the crazy-paved path on the side. And even in a kind of luminous darkness from the white of the breakers ahead, he saw why the bungalow showed no lights.

All the curtains were drawn on the windows—on this side, at least.

When Dan hurried round to the front door, he was almost running. He banged the iron knocker on the door, then hammered it again. As he glanced over his shoulder, another flash of lightning paled the sky to the west.

It showed him the sweep of gray sand. It showed black water snakily edged with foam. In the middle of the beach, unearthly, stood the small natural rock formation—shaped like a low-backed armchair, eternally facing out to sea—which for centuries had been known as King Arthur's Chair.

The white eye of the lightning closed. Distantly there was a shock of thunder.

This whole bungalow couldn't be deserted! Even if Edmund Ireton and Toby Curtis were at the former's house some distance along the coast, Brenda herself must be here. And Joyce Ray. And the two maids.

Dan stopped hammering the knocker. He groped for and found the knob of the door.

The door was unlocked.

He opened it on brightness. In the hall, rather overdecorated like so many of Brenda's possessions, several lamps shone on gaudy furniture and a polished floor. But the hall was empty too.

With the wind whisking and whistling at his back Dan went in and kicked the door shut behind him. He had no time to give a hail. At the back of the hall a door opened. Joyce Ray, Brenda's cousin, walked toward him, her arms hanging limply at her sides and her enormous eyes like a sleepwalker's.

"Then you did get here," said Joyce, moistening dry lips. "You did get here, after all."

"I—"

Dan stopped. The sight of her brought a new realization. It didn't explain his uneasiness or his fear—but it did explain much.

Joyce was the quiet one, the dark one, the unobtrusive one, with her glossy black hair and her subdued elegance. But she was the poor relation, and Brenda never let her forget it. Dan merely stood and stared at her. Suddenly Joyce's eyes lost their sleepwalker's look. They were gray eyes, with very black lashes; they grew alive and vivid, as if she could read his mind.

"Joyce," he blurted, "I've just understood something. And I never understood it before. But I've got to tell—"

"Stop!" Joyce cried.

Her mouth twisted. She put up a hand as if to shade her eyes.

"I know what you want to say," she went on. "But you're not to say it! Do you hear me?"

"Joyce, I don't know why we're standing here yelling at each other. Anyway, I—I didn't mean to tell you. Not yet, anyway. I mean, I must tell Brenda—"

"You can't tell Brenda!" Joyce cried.

"What's that?"

"You can't tell her anything, ever again," said Joyce. "Brenda's dead."

There are some words which at first do not even shock or stun. You just don't believe them. They can't be true. Very carefully Dan Fraser put his suitcase down on the floor and straightened up again.

"The police," said Joyce, swallowing hard, "have been here since early this morning. They're not here now. They've taken her away to the mortuary. That's where she'll sleep tonight."

Still Dan said nothing.

"Mr.—Mr. Edmund Ireton," Joyce went on, "has been here ever since it happened. So has Toby Curtis. So, fortunately, has a man named Dr. Gideon Fell. Dr. Fell's a bumbling old duffer, a very learned man or something. He's a friend of the police; he's kind;

he's helped soften things. All the same, Dan, if you'd been here last night—"

"I couldn't get away. I told Brenda so."

"Yes, I know all that talk about hard-working journalists. But if you'd only been here, Dan, it might not have happened at all."

"Joyce, for God's sake!"

Then there was a silence in the bright, quiet room. A stricken look crept into Joyce's eyes.

"Dan, I'm sorry. I'm terribly sorry. I was feeling dreadful and so, I suppose, I had to take it out on the first person handy."

"That's all right. But how did she die?" Then desperately he began to surmise. "Wait, I've got it! She went out to swim early this morning, just as usual? She's been diving off those rocks on the headland again? And—"

"No," said Joyce. "She was strangled."

"*Strangled?*"

What Joyce tried to say was "murdered." Her mouth shook and faltered round the syllables; she couldn't say them; her thoughts, it seemed, shied back and ran from the very word. But she looked at Dan steadily.

"Brenda went out to swim early this morning, yes."

"Well?"

"At least, she must have. I didn't see her. I was still asleep in that back bedroom she always gives me. Anyway, she went down there in a red swim suit and a white beach robe."

Automatically Dan's eyes moved over to an oil painting above the fireplace. Painted by a famous R.A., it showed a scene from classical antiquity; it was called *The Lovers*, and left little to the imagination. It had always been Brenda's favorite because the female figure in the picture looked so much like her.

"Well!" said Joyce, throwing out her hands. "You know what Brenda always does. She takes off her beach robe and spreads it out over King Arthur's Chair. She sits down in the chair and smokes a cigarette and looks out at the sea before she goes into the water.

"The beach robe was still in that rock chair," Joyce continued with an effort, "when I came downstairs at half-past seven. But Brenda wasn't. She hadn't even put on her bathing cap. Somebody had strangled her with that silk scarf she wore with the beach robe. It was twisted so tightly into her neck they couldn't get it out. She was lying on the sand in front of the chair, on her back, in the red swim suit, with her face black and swollen. You could see her clearly from the terrace."

Dan glanced at the flesh tints of *The Lovers*, then quickly looked away.

Joyce, the cool and competent, was holding herself under restraint.

"I can only thank my lucky stars," she burst out, "I didn't run out there. I mean, from the flagstones of the lowest terrace out across the sand. They stopped me."

" 'They' stopped you? Who?"

"Mr. Ireton and Toby. Or, rather, Mr. Ireton did; Toby wouldn't have thought of it."

"But—"

"Toby, you see, had come over here a little earlier. But he was at the back of the bungalow, practising with a .22 target rifle. I heard him once. Mr. Ireton had just got there. All three of us walked out on the terrace at once. And saw her."

"Listen, Joyce. What difference does it make whether or not you ran out across the sand? Why were you so lucky they stopped you?"

"Because if they hadn't, the police might have said I did it."

"Did it?"

"Killed Brenda," Joyce answered clearly. "In all that stretch of sand, Dan, there weren't any footprints except Brenda's own."

"Now hold on!" he protested. "She—she was killed with that scarf of hers?"

"Oh, yes. The police and even Dr. Fell don't doubt that."

"Then how could anybody, anybody at all, go out across the sand and come back without leaving a footprint?"

"That's just it. The police don't know and they can't guess. That's why they're in a flat spin, and Dr. Fell will be here again tonight."

In her desperate attempt to speak lightly, as if all this didn't matter, Joyce failed. Her face was white. But again the expression of the dark-fringed eyes changed, and she hesitated.

"Dan—"

"Yes?"

"You do understand, don't you, why I was so upset when you came charging in and said what you did?"

"Yes, of course."

"Whatever you had to tell me, or thought you had to tell me—"

"About—us?"

"About anything! You do see that you must forget it and not mention it again? Not ever?"

"I see why I can't mention it now. With Brenda dead, it wouldn't even be decent to think of it." He could not keep his eyes off that mocking picture. "But is the future dead too? If I happen to have been an idiot and thought I was head over heels gone on Brenda when all the time it was really—"

"Dan!"

There were five doors opening into the gaudy hall, which had too many mirrors. Joyce whirled round to look at every door, as if she feared an ambush behind each.

"For heaven's sake keep your voice down," she begged. "Practically every word that's said can be heard all over the house. I said never, and I meant it. If you'd spoken a week ago, even twenty-four hours ago, it might have been different. Do you think I didn't want you to? But now it's too late!"

"Why?"

"May I answer that question?" interrupted a new, dry, rather quizzical voice.

Dan had taken a step toward her, intensely conscious of her attractiveness. He stopped, burned with embarrassment, as one of the five doors opened.

Mr. Edmund Ireton, shortish and thin and dandified in his middle fifties, emerged with his usual briskness. There was not much gray in his polished black hair. His face was a benevolent satyr's.

"Forgive me," he said.

Behind him towered Toby Curtis, heavy and handsome and fair-haired, in a bulky tweed jacket. Toby began to speak, but Mr. Ireton's gesture silenced him before he could utter a sound.

"Forgive me," he repeated. "But what Joyce says is quite true. Every word can be overheard here, even with the rain pouring down. If you go on shouting and Dr. Fell hears it, you will land that girl in serious danger."

"Danger?" demanded Toby Curtis. He had to clear his throat. "What danger could Dan get her into?"

Mr. Ireton, immaculate in flannels and shirt and thin pullover, stalked to the mantelpiece. He stared up hard at *The Lovers* before turning round.

"The Psalmist tells us," he said dryly, "that all is vanity. Has none of you ever noticed—God forgive me for saying so—that Brenda's most outstanding trait was her vanity?"

His glance flashed toward Joyce, who abruptly turned away and pressed her hands over her face.

"Appalling vanity. Scratch that vanity deeply enough and our dearest Brenda would have committed murder."

"Aren't you getting this backwards?" asked Dan. "Brenda didn't commit any murder. It was Brenda—"

"Ah!" Mr. Ireton pounced. "And there might be a lesson in that, don't you think?"

"Look here, you're not saying she strangled herself with her own scarf?"

"No—but hear what I do say. Our Brenda, no doubt, had many passions and many fancies. But there was only one man she loved or ever wanted to marry. It was not Mr. Dan Fraser."

"Then who was it?" asked Toby.

"You."

Toby's amazement was too genuine to be assumed. The color drained out of his face. Once more he had to clear his throat.

"So help me," he said, "I never knew it! I never imagined—"

"No, of course you didn't," Mr. Ireton said even more dryly. A goatish amusement flashed across his face and was gone. "Brenda, as a rule, could get any man she chose. So she turned Mr. Fraser's head and became engaged to him. It was to sting you, Mr. Curtis, to make you jealous. And you never noticed. While all the time Joyce Ray and Dan Fraser were eating their hearts out for each other; and *he* never noticed either."

Edmund Ireton wheeled round.

"You may lament my bluntness, Mr. Fraser. You may want to wring my neck, as I see you do. But can you deny one word I say?"

"No." In honesty Dan could not deny it.

"Well! Then be very careful when you face the police, both of you, or they will see it too. Joyce already has a strong motive. She is Brenda's only relative, and inherits Brenda's money. If they learn she wanted Brenda's fiancé, they will have her in the dock for murder."

"That's enough!" blurted Dan, who dared not look at Joyce. "You've made it clear. All right, stop there!"

"Oh, I had intended to stop. If you are such fools that you won't help yourselves, I must help you. That's all."

It was Toby Curtis who strode forward.

"Dan, don't let him bluff you!" Toby said. "In the first place, they can't arrest anybody for this. You weren't here. I know—"

"I've heard about it, Toby."

"Look," insisted Toby. "When the police finished measuring and photographing and taking casts of Brenda's footprints, I did some measuring myself."

Edmund Ireton smiled. "Are you attempting to solve this mystery, Mr. Curtis?"

"I didn't say that." Toby spoke coolly. "But I might have a question or two for you. Why have you had your knife into me all day?"

"Frankly, Mr. Curtis, because I envy you."

"You—what?"

"So far as women are concerned, young man, I have not your advantages. *I* had no romantic boyhood on a veldt-farm in South Africa. *I* never learned to drive a span of oxen and flick a fly off the leader's ear with my whip. I was never taught to be a spectacular horseman and rifle shot."

"Oh, turn it up!"

" 'Turn it up?' Ah, I see. And was that the sinister question you had for me?"

"No. Not yet. You're too tricky."

"My profoundest thanks."

"Look, Dan," Toby insisted. "You've seen that rock formation they call King Arthur's Chair?"

"Toby, I've seen it fifty times," Dan said. "But I still don't understand—"

"And I don't understand," suddenly interrupted Joyce, without turning round, "why they made me sit there where Brenda had been sitting. It was horrible."

"Oh, they were only reconstructing the crime." Toby spoke rather grandly. "But the question, Dan, is how anybody came near that chair without leaving a footprint?"

"Quite."

"Nobody could have," Toby said just as grandly. "The murderer, for instance, couldn't have come from the direction of the sea. Why? Because the highest point at high tide, where the water might have blotted out footprints, is more than twenty feet in front of the chair. More than twenty feet!"

"Er—one moment," said Mr. Ireton, twitching up a finger. "Surely Inspector Tregellis said the murderer must have crept up and caught her from the back? Before she knew it?"

"That won't do either. From the flagstones of the terrace to the back of the chair is at least twenty feet, too. Well, Dan? Do you see any way out of that one?"

Dan, not normally slow-witted, was so concentrating on Joyce that he could think of little else. She was cut off from him, drifting away from him, forever out of reach just when he had found her. But he tried to think.

"Well . . . could somebody have jumped there?"

"Ho!" scoffed Toby, who was himself a broad jumper and knew better. "That was the first thing they thought of."

"And that's out, too?"

"Definitely. An Olympic champion in good form might have done it, if he'd had any place for a running start and any place to land. But he hadn't. There was no mark in the sand. He couldn't have landed on the chair, strangled Brenda at his leisure, and then hopped back like a jumping bean. Now could he?"

"But somebody did it, Toby! It happened!"

"How?"

"I don't know."

"You seem rather proud of this, Mr. Curtis," Edmund Ireton said smoothly.

"Proud?" exclaimed Toby, losing color again.

"These romantic boyhoods—"

Toby did not lose his temper. But he had declared war.

"All right, gaffer. I've been very grateful for your hospitality, at that bungalow of yours, when we've come down here for weekends. All the same, you've been going on for hours about who I am and what I am. Who are you?"

"I beg your pardon?"

"For two or three years," Toby said, "you've been hanging about with us. Especially with Brenda and Joyce. Who are you? What are you?"

"I am an observer of life," Mr. Ireton answered tranquilly. "A student of human nature. And—shall I say?—a courtesy uncle to both young ladies."

"Is that all you were? To either of them?"

"Toby!" exclaimed Joyce, shocked out of her fear.

She whirled round, her gaze going instinctively to Dan, then back to Toby.

"Don't worry, old girl," said Toby, waving his hand at her. "This is no reflection on you." He kept looking steadily at Mr. Ireton.

"Continue," Mr. Ireton said politely.

"You claim Joyce is in danger. She isn't in any danger at all," said Toby, "as long as the police don't know how Brenda was strangled."

"They will discover it, Mr. Curtis. Be sure they will discover it!"

"You're trying to protect Joyce?"

"Naturally."

"And that's why you warned Dan not to say he was in love with her?"

"Of course. What else?"

Toby straightened up, his hand inside the bulky tweed jacket.

"Then why didn't you take him outside, rain or no, and tell him on the quiet? Why did you shout out that Dan was in love with

Joyce, and she was in love with him, and give 'em a motive for the whole house to hear?"

Edmund Ireton opened his mouth, and shut it again.

It was a blow under the guard, all the more unexpected because it came from Toby Curtis.

Mr. Ireton stood motionless under the painting of *The Lovers*. The expression of the pictured Brenda, elusive and mocking, no longer matched his own. Whereupon, while nerves were strained and still nobody spoke, Dan Fraser realized that there was a dead silence because the rain had stopped.

Small night-noises, the creak of woodwork or a drip of water from the eaves, intensified the stillness. Then they heard footsteps, as heavy as those of an elephant, slowly approaching behind another of the doors. The footfalls, heavy and slow and creaking, brought a note of doom.

Into the room, wheezing and leaning on a stick, lumbered a man so enormous that he had to maneuver himself sideways through the door.

His big mop of gray-streaked hair had tumbled over one ear. His eyeglasses, with a broad black ribbon, were stuck askew on his nose. His big face would ordinarily have been red and beaming, with chuckles animating several chins. Now it was only absent-minded, his bandit's moustache outthrust.

"Aha!" he said in a rumbling voice. He blinked at Dan with an air of refreshed interest. "I think you must be Mr. Fraser, the last of this rather curious weekend party? H'm. Yes. Your obedient servant, sir. I am Gideon Fell."

Dr. Fell wore a black cloak as big as a tent and carried a shovel-hat in his other hand. He tried to bow and make a flourish with his stick, endangering all the furniture near him.

The others stood very still. Fear was as palpable as the scent after rain.

"Yes, I've heard of you," said Dan. His voice rose in spite of himself. "But you're rather far from home, aren't you? I suppose you had some—er—antiquarian interest in King Arthur's Chair?"

Still Dr. Fell blinked at him. For a second it seemed that chuckles would jiggle his chins and waistcoat, but he only shook his head.

"Antiquarian interest? My dear sir!" Dr. Fell wheezed gently. "If there were any association with a semi-legendary King Arthur, it would be at Tintagel much farther south. No, I was here on holiday. This morning Inspector Tregellis fascinated me with the story of a fantastic murder. I returned tonight for my own reasons."

Mr. Ireton, at ease again, matched the other's courtesy. "May I ask what these reasons were?"

"First, I wished to question the two maids. They have a room at the back, as Miss Ray has; and this afternoon, you may remember, they were still rather hysterical."

"And that is all?"

"H'mf. Well, no." Dr. Fell scowled. "Second, I wanted to detain all of you here for an hour or two. Third, I must make sure of the motive for this crime. And I am happy to say that I have made very sure."

Joyce could not control herself. "Then you did overhear everything!"

"Eh?"

"Every word that man said!"

Despite Dan's signals, Joyce nodded toward Mr. Ireton and poured out the words. "But I swear I hadn't anything to do with Brenda's death. What I told you today was perfectly true: I don't want her money and I won't touch it. As for my—my private affairs," and Joyce's face flamed, "everybody seems to know all about them except Dan and me. Please, please pay no attention to what that man has been saying."

Dr. Fell blinked at her in an astonishment which changed to vast distress.

"But, my dear young lady!" he rumbled. "We never for a moment believed you did. No, no! Archons of Athens, no!" exclaimed Dr. Fell, as though at incredible absurdity. "As for what your friend Mr. Ireton may have been saying, I did not hear it. I suspect it was only what he told me today, and it did supply the motive. But it was not your motive."

"Please, is this true? You're not trying to trap me?"

"Do I really strike you," Dr. Fell asked gently, "as being that sort of person? Nothing was more unlikely than that you killed your cousin, especially in the way she was killed."

"Do you know how she was killed?"

"Oh, *that*," grunted Dr. Fell, waving the point away too. "That was the simplest part of the whole business."

He lumbered over, reflected in the mirrors, and put down stick and shovel-hat on a table. Afterward he faced them with a mixture of distress and apology.

"It may surprise you," he said, "that an old scatterbrain like myself can observe anything at all. But I have an unfair advantage over the police. I began life as a schoolmaster: I have had more experience with habitual liars. Hang it all, think!"

"Of what?"

"The facts!" said Dr. Fell, making a hideous face. "According to the maids, Sonia and Dolly, Miss Brenda Lestrange went down to swim at ten minutes to seven this morning. Both Dolly and Sonia were awake, but did not get up. Some eight or ten minutes later, Mr. Toby Curtis began practising with a target rifle some distance away behind the bungalow."

"Don't look at me!" exclaimed Toby. "That rifle has nothing to do with it. Brenda wasn't shot."

"Sir," said Dr. Fell with much patience, "I am aware of that."

"Then what are you hinting at?"

"Sir," said Dr. Fell, "you will oblige me if you too don't regard every question as a trap. I have a trap for the murderer, and the murderer alone. You fired a number of shots—the maids heard you and saw you." He turned to Joyce. "I believe you heard too?"

"I heard one shot," answered the bewildered Joyce, "as I told Dan. About seven o'clock, when I got up and dressed."

"Did you look out of the windows?"

"No."

"What happened to that rifle afterwards? Is it here now?"

"No," Toby almost yelled. "I took it back to Ireton's after we found Brenda. But if the rifle had nothing to do with it, and I had nothing to do with it, then what the hell's the point?"

Dr. Fell did not reply for a moment. Then he made another hideous face. "We know," he rumbled, "that Brenda Lestrange wore a beach robe, a bathing suit, and a heavy silk scarf knotted round her neck. Miss Ray?"

"Y-yes?"

"I am not precisely an authority on women's clothes," said Dr. Fell. "As a rule I should notice nothing odd unless I passed Madge Wildfire or Lady Godiva. I have seen men wear a scarf with a beach robe, but is it customary for women to wear a scarf as well?"

There was a pause.

"No, of course it isn't," said Joyce. "I can't speak for everybody, but I never do. It was just one of Brenda's fancies. She always did."

"Aha!" said Dr. Fell. "The murderer was counting on that."

"On what?"

"On her known conduct. Let me show you rather a grisly picture of a murder."

Dr. Fell's eyes were squeezed shut. From inside his cloak and pocket he fished out an immense meerschaum pipe. Firmly under the impression that he had filled and lighted the pipe, he put the stem in his mouth and drew at it.

"Miss Lestrange," he said, "goes down to the beach. She takes off her robe. Remember that, it's very important. She spreads out the robe in King Arthur's Chair and sits down. She is still wearing the scarf, knotted tightly in a broad band round her neck. She is about the same height as you, Miss Ray. She is held there, at the height of her shoulders, by a curving rock formation deeply bedded in sand."

Dr. Fell paused and opened his eyes.

"The murderer, we believe, catches her from the back. She sees and hears nothing until she is seized. Intense pressure on the carotid arteries, here at either side of the neck under the chin, will strike her unconscious within seconds and dead within minutes. When her body is released, it should fall straight forward. Instead, what happens?"

To Dan, full of relief ever since danger had seemed to leave Joyce, it was as if a shutter had flown open in his brain.

"She was lying on her back," Dan said. "Joyce told me so. Brenda was lying flat on her back with her head towards the sea. And that means—"

"Yes?"

"It means she was twisted or spun round in some way when she fell. It has something to do with that infernal scarf—I've thought so from the first. Dr. Fell! Was Brenda killed with the scarf?"

"In one sense, yes. In another sense, no."

"You can't have it both ways! Either she was killed with the scarf, or she wasn't."

"Not necessarily," said Dr. Fell.

"Then let's all retire to a loony bin," Dan suggested, "because nothing makes any sense at all. The murderer still couldn't have walked out there without leaving tracks. Finally, I agree with Toby: what's the point of the rifle? How does a .22 rifle figure in all this?"

"Because of its sound."

Dr. Fell took the pipe out of his mouth. Dan wondered why he had ever thought the learned doctor's eyes were vague. Magnified behind the glasses on the broad black ribbon, they were not vague at all.

"A .22 rifle," he went on in his big voice, "has a distinctive noise. Fired in the open air or anywhere else, it sounds exactly like the noise made by the real instrument used in this crime."

"Real instrument? What noise?"

"The crack of a blacksnake whip," replied Dr. Fell.

Edmund Ireton, looking very tired and ten years older, went over and sat down in an easy chair. Toby Curtis took one step backward, then another.

"In South Africa," said Dr. Fell, "I have never seen the very long whip which drivers of long ox spans use. But in America I have seen the blacksnake whip, and it can be twenty-four feet long. You yourselves must have watched it used in a variety turn on the stage."

Dr. Fell pointed his pipe at them.

"Remember?" he asked. "The user of the whip stands some distance away facing his girl-assistant. There is a vicious crack. The end of the whip coils two or three times round the girl's neck. She is not hurt. But she would be in difficulties if he pulled the whip towards him. She would be in grave danger if she were held back and could not move.

"Somebody planned a murder with a whip like that. He came here early in the morning. The whip, coiled round his waist, was hidden by a loose and bulky tweed jacket. Please observe the jacket Toby Curtis is wearing now."

Toby's voice went high when he screeched out one word. It may have been protest, defiance, a jeer, or all three.

"Stop this!" cried Joyce, who had again turned away.

"Continue, I beg," Mr. Ireton said.

"In the dead hush of morning," said Dr. Fell, "he could not hide the loud crack of the whip. But what could he do?"

"He could mask it," said Edmund Ireton.

"Just that! He was always practising with a .22 rifle. So he fired several shots, behind the bungalow, to establish his presence. Afterwards nobody would notice when the crack of the whip—that single, isolated 'shot' heard by Miss Ray—only seemed to come from behind the house."

"Then, actually, he was—?"

"On the terrace, twenty feet behind a victim held immovable in the curve of a stone chair. The end of the whip coiled round the scarf. Miss Lestrange's breath was cut off instantly. Under the pull of a powerful arm she died in seconds.

"On the stage, you recall, a lift and twist dislodges the whip from the girl-assistant's neck. Toby Curtis had a harder task; the scarf was so embedded in her neck that she seemed to have been strangled with it. He *could* dislodge it. But only with a powerful whirl and lift of the arm which spun her up and round, to fall face upwards. The whip snaked back to him with no trace in the sand. Afterwards he had only to take the whip back to Mr. Ireton's house, under pretext of returning the rifle. He had committed a murder which, in his vanity, he thought undetectable. That's all."

"But it can't be all!" said Dan. "Why should Toby have killed her? His motive—"

"His motive was offended vanity. Mr. Edmund Ireton as good as told you so, I fancy. He had certainly hinted as much to me."

Edmund Ireton rose shakily from the chair.

"I am no judge or executioner," he said. "I—I am detached from life. I only observe. If I guessed why this was done—"

"You could never speak straight out?" Dr. Fell asked sardonically.

"No!"

"And yet that was the tragic irony of the whole affair. Miss Lestrange wanted Toby Curtis, as he wanted her. But, being a woman, her pretense of indifference and contempt was too good. He believed it. Scratch her vanity deeply enough and she would have committed murder. Scratch *his* vanity deeply enough—"

"Lies!" said Toby.

"Look at him, all of you!" said Dr. Fell. "Even when he's accused of murder, he can't take his eyes off a mirror."

"Lies!"

"She laughed at him," the big voice went on, "and so she had to die. Brutally and senselessly he killed a girl who would have been his for the asking. That is what I meant by tragic irony."

Toby had retreated across the room until his back bumped against a wall. Startled, he looked behind him; he had banged against another mirror.

"Lies!" he kept repeating. "You can talk and talk and talk. But there's not a single damned thing you can prove!"

"Sir," inquired Dr. Fell, "are you sure?"

"Yes!"

"I warned you," said Dr. Fell, "that I returned tonight partly to detain all of you for an hour or so. It gave Inspector Tregellis time to search Mr. Ireton's house, and the Inspector has since returned. I further warned you that I questioned the maids, Sonia and Dolly, who today were only incoherent. My dear sir, you underestimate your personal attractions."

Now it was Joyce who seemed to understand. But she did not speak.

"Sonia, it seems," and Dr. Fell looked hard at Toby, "has quite a fondness for you. When she heard that last isolated 'shot' this morning, she looked out of the window again. You weren't there. This was so strange that she ran out to the front terrace to discover where you were. She saw you."

The door by which Dr. Fell had entered was still open. His voice lifted and echoed through the hall.

"Come in, Sonia!" he called. "After all, you are a witness to the murder. You, Inspector, had better come in too."

Toby Curtis blundered back, but there was no way out. There was only a brief glimpse of Sonia's swollen, tear-stained face. Past her marched a massive figure in uniform, carrying what he had found hidden in the other house.

Inspector Tregellis was reflected everywhere in the mirrors, with the long coils of the whip over his arm. And he seemed to be carrying not a whip but a coil of rope—gallows rope.

SECRET SERVICE STORIES

Strictly Diplomatic

Now that he was nearly at the end of his rest-cure, Dermot had never felt so well in his life.

He leaned back in the wicker chair, flexing his muscles. He breathed deeply. Below him the flattish lands between France and Belgium sloped to the river: a slow Flemish river dark green with the reflection of its banks. Half a mile away he could see the houses of the town, with the great glass roof of the spa smoky in autumn sunshine. Behind him—at the end of the arbor—was the back of the hotel, now denuded of its awnings.

They had taken down the awnings; they were closing up many of the bedrooms. Only a few guests now pottered about the terrace. A crisp tang had come into the air: work, and the thunder of London again, now loomed up as a pleasant prospect. Once, hardly a month ago, it had been a nightmare of buses charging straight at you, like houses loose; a place where nerves snapped, and you started to run.

Even with that noise in his ears, he had not wanted to go away.

"But I can't take a holiday now!" he had told the doctor.

"Holiday?" snorted the doctor. "Do you call it a holiday? Your trouble is plain overwork, a complaint we don't often get nowadays. Why don't you relax? Not hard up, are you?"

"No, it isn't that."

"You're too conscientious," the doctor had said, rather enviously.

"No. It's not a virtue," said Dermot, as honestly as he could. "I can't help it. Every second I'm away from work, I'm worrying about it until I get back. I'm built like that. I can't relax. I can't even get drunk."

The doctor grunted.

"Ever try falling in love?"

"Not since I was nineteen. And, anyway, it's not something you can take down like a box of pills and dose yourself with. Or at least I can't."

"Well," said the doctor, surveying him, "I know a rising barrister who's going to come a cropper unless you get out of this. Now I warn you. You get off to the Continent this week. There's a spa I know—Ile St. Cathérine. The waters won't do you any harm; and the golf will do you good."

Here the doctor, who was an old friend of Andrew Dermot's, grinned raffishly.

"What you want," he added, "is adventure. In the grand manner. I hear there's a fenced-off area near Ile St. Cathérine, bayonets and all. The casino is probably full of beautiful slant-eyed spies with jade earrings. Forget you're turning into such a mossback. Pick up one of the beautiful slant-eyed spies, and go on the razzle-dazzle with her. It'll do you all the good in the world."

Alone on the lawn behind his hotel, Dermot laughed aloud. Old Foggy had been right, in a way. But he had gone one less or one better than that. He had fallen in love.

Anyone less like a slant-eyed spy than Betty Weatherill would be difficult to imagine. In fact even the tension which tautened nerves in the rest of Europe did not exist in Ile St. Cathérine. It was a fat, friendly, rather stodgy sort of place. Looking round the spa—where fountains fell, and people got very excited on the weighing-machines—Dermot wondered at old Foggy's notion of bayonets. He felt soothed, and free. Bicycle bells tinkled in the streets under once-gilded houses. At night, when you ordered thin wine by the glass, a band played beneath lights in the trees. A mild flutter in roulette at the casino caused excitement; and one Belgian burgher was caught bringing his supper in a paper packet.

Dermot first saw Betty Weatherill on the morning after his arrival.

It was at breakfast. There were not many guests at the hotel: a fat Dutchman eating cheese for breakfast, half a dozen English people, a foreign envoy, a subdued French couple. And, of course, the sturdy girl who sat alone at the sun-steeped table by the windows.

Dermot's nerves were still raw from the journey. When he first saw her he felt a twinge of what he thought was envy at her sheer health. It flashed out at him. He had an impression of a friendly mouth, a sun-tanned complexion; of eagerness, and even naïveté. It disturbed him like the clattering coffee-cups. He kept looking round at her, and looking round again, though he did not understand why.

He played execrable golf that day.

He saw her again next morning. They ran into each other buying stamps at the cash desk. They both smiled slightly, and Dermot felt embarrassed. He had been trying to remember whether the color of her hair was fair or chestnut; it was, he saw, a light brown. That afternoon his golf was even worse. It was absurd that he, thirty-five years old, should seem as stale and crumpled as an old poster against a wall. He was a nerve-ridden fool. And he fell to thinking of her again.

On the following day they went so far as to say good morning. On the third day he took his nerve in both hands, and plumped down at the breakfast table next to hers.

"I can't do it," he heard her say, half-laughing.

The words gave him a start. Not a ladies' man, this move of his had struck him as distinctly daring. Yet he felt the communication between them, an uncomfortable awareness of each other's presence. He looked up, to find her eyes fixed on him.

"Do what?" he asked quickly.

"Manage Continental breakfasts," she answered, as though they were old friends discussing a problem of mutual importance. "I know I shouldn't, but every day I order bacon and eggs."

After that their acquaintance was off at a gallop.

Her name was Betty Weatherill. She was twenty-eight, and came from Brighton. She had been a schoolmistress (incongruous idea); but she had come into a small inheritance and, as she confessed, was blowing part of it. He had never met a girl who seemed so absolutely right: in what she said, in what she did, in her response to any given remark.

That afternoon they went to the fair and ate hot dogs and rode round and round on the wooden horses to the panting music of an electric piano. That night they dressed for the casino; and Andrew Dermot, shuffling roulette-counters, felt no end of an experienced gay-dog. And the knowledge came to him, with a kind of shock, "Good lord, I'm alive."

Betty was popular at the hotel. The proprietor, Monsieur Gant, knew her quite well and was fond of her. Even the fat Dr. Vanderver, of the Sylvanian Embassy, gave her a hoarse chuckle of appreciation whenever she went by. Not that she had no difficulties. There was, it appeared, some trouble about her passport. She had several times to go to the prefecture of police—from which she emerged flushed, and as near angry as it was possible for her to be.

As for Dermot, he was in love and he knew it. That was why he exulted when he sat by the tea-table on the lawn behind the hotel, at half-past five on that lazy, veiled autumn afternoon, waiting for Betty to join him. The lawn was dotted with little tables, but he was alone. The remains of tea and sandwiches were piled on a tray. Dermot was replete; no outside alarms troubled Ile St. Cathérine; no black emblems threw shadows.

This was just before he received the greatest shock of his life.

"Hello!" said Betty. "Sorry I'm late." She came hurrying out of the arbor, with the breathless smile she always wore when she was excited. She glanced quickly round the lawn, deserted except for a waitress slapping at crumbs. Dermot got up.

"You're not late," he told her. "But you swore to me you were going to have tea in town, so I went ahead." He looked at her suspiciously. "Did you?"

"Did I what?"

"Have tea."

"Yes, of course."

For no reason that he could analyze, a chill of uneasiness came to Dermot. His nightmares were cured. But it was as though an edge of the nightmare returned. Why? Only because the atmosphere suddenly seemed wrong, because the expression of her eyes was wrong. He drew out a chair for her.

"Sure you wouldn't like another cup? Or a sandwich?"

"Well—"

Now he thought he must be a fool reading huge meanings into trifles. But the impression persisted. He gave an order to the waitress, who removed the tea-tray and disappeared into the arbor. Betty had taken a cigarette out of her handbag; but, when he tried to light it for her, the cigarette slipped out of her fingers, and rolled on the table.

"Oh, damn," she whispered. Now he was looking into her eyes from a short distance away; they seemed the eyes of a slightly older, wiser woman. They were hazel eyes, the whites very clear against a sun-tanned face. The heavy lids blinked.

"I want to know what's wrong," Dermot said.

"There's nothing wrong," said Betty, shaking her head. "Only— I wanted to talk to you. I'm afraid I've got to leave here."

"When?"

"Tonight."

Dermot sat up. It seemed to him that there was a stranger sitting across from him, and that all his plans were toppling.

"If you must, you must," he said. "But I've got to go myself at the beginning of the week. I thought we were going to leave together."

"I can't. Very shortly"—she spoke with some intensity—"I hope I can explain to you what a beast I am. All I can tell you now is that it's not altogether safe for me to be here."

"Safe? In this place?"

Betty was not listening. She was wearing white, as he always remembered afterwards, with a white handbag. Again she had opened this handbag, and was going through it in something of a hurry.

"Derry." She spoke sharply. "You haven't seen my compact, have you? The white ivory one with the red band?" She looked round. "It didn't fall out when I opened my handbag before?"

"No, I don't think so. I didn't see it."

"I must have left it back in my room. Please excuse me. I'll be back in half a tick."

And she got to her feet, snapped shut the catch of the handbag.

Dermot also got up. It would not be fair to say that he exploded. He was a mild-mannered man who arrived at all emotions with difficulty. But in the past few minutes he felt that a door had opened on a world he could not understand.

"Look here, Betty," he said. "I don't know what's got into you; but I insist on knowing. If there's anything wrong, just tell me and we'll put it right. If—"

"I'll be back in a moment," she assured him.

And, disregarding the hand he put out, she hurried back through the arbor.

Dermot sat down heavily, and stared after her. A veiled sun had turned the sky to gray, making dingy the cloths of the little tables on the lawn. The cloths fluttered under a faint breeze.

He contemplated the arbor, which was a very special sort of arbor. Monsieur Gant, the proprietor of the Hotel Suchard, had imported it from Italy and was very proud of it. Stretching back a full twenty yards to the rear terrace of the hotel, it made a sort of tunnel composed of tough interlaced vines which in summer were heavy with purplish-pink blossom. A line of tables ran beside it, with lights from above. Inside the arbor, at night, Chinese lanterns hung from the roof. It was one of the romantic features of the hotel. But at the moment—cramped, unlighted, hooded with thick foliage—it was a tunnel which suggested unpleasant images.

"A good place for a murder," Betty had once laughed.

Andrew Dermot could hear his watch ticking. He wished she would come back.

He lit a cigarette and smoked it to a stump; but she had not returned. He got to his feet, stamping on the chilling grass. For the first time he glanced across the tea-table at Betty's empty chair. It was a wicker chair. And, lying on the seat in plain view, was a white ivory compact with a red band.

So that was it! She had been too much upset to notice the compact, of course. She was probably still searching her room for it.

He picked up the compact and went after her.

Inside the arbor it was almost dark, but chinks and glimmers of light flickered through interlaced vines and showed him an arched tunnel some ten feet high, with a floor of packed sand. There was a stagnant smell of dying blossom; the Judas tree, did they call it? Obscurely, he was relieved to find the gnat-stung arbor empty. He hurried along its length to the arch of light at the end, and emerged on a red-tiled terrace where there were more tables under the windows.

"Good eefening, Mr. Dermot," said an affable voice.

Dermot checked his rush.

He almost stumbled over Dr. Henrik Vanderver of the Sylvanian

Embassy, who was sitting near the arbor, smoking a cigar with relish, and looking at him through thick-lensed spectacles.

"Ha, ha, ha!" said Dr. Vanderver, laughing uproariously and for no apparent reason, as was his custom.

"Good evening, Dr. Vanderver," said Dermot. His uneasiness had gone; he felt again a nerve-ridden fool. "Sorry to barge into you like that. Is Miss Weatherill down yet?"

Dr. Vanderver was proud of his English.

"Down?" he repeated, drawing down his eyebrows as though to illustrate.

"From her room, I mean."

"De young lady," said Vanderver, "iss with you. I have seen her go through dere"—he pointed to the arbor—"fifteen, twenty minutes ago."

"Yes, I know. But she came back here to get a compact."

Vanderver was now anxious about his English.

"Please?" he prompted, cupping his hand behind his ear.

"I said she came back here to get a compact. You know. This kind of thing." Dermot held it up. "She walked back through the arbor—"

"My friend," said Vanderver with sudden passion, "I do not know if I have understood you. Nobody has come back through this arbor while I am sitting here."

"But that's impossible."

"Please?"

Dermot thought he saw the explanation. "You mean you haven't been sitting here all the time?"

"My friend," said Vanderver, taking out a watch and shaking it, "I am sitting here one hour more—more!—where I sit always and smoke my cigar before I dress. Yes?"

"Well, Doctor?"

"I have seen the young lady go through, yes. But I have not seen her come back. I haf not seen nobody. In all dat time the only liffing soul I see on this terrace is the maid which gather up your tea-tray and bring it back here."

The terrace, always dark in the shadow of the arbor, was growing more dusky.

"Dr. Vanderver, listen to me." Dermot spoke coldly and sharply; he found Vanderver's thick-lensed spectacles turning on him with hypnotic effect. "That is not what I mean. I remember the maid going back through the arbor with the tray. But Miss Weatherill was with me then. I mean later. L-a-t-e-r, several minutes later. You saw Miss Weatherill come out through here about ten minutes ago, didn't you?"

"No."

"But you must have! I saw her go into the arbor on my side, and I never took my eyes off the entrance. She isn't in the arbor now; see for yourself. She must have come out here."

"So!" said Vanderver, tapping the table with magnificent dignity. "Now I tell you something. I do not know what you think has happened to the young lady. Perhaps de goblins ketch her, yes? Perhaps she dissolved to electrons and bust, yes?" Dark blood suffused his face. "Now I will haf no more of this. I settle it. I tell you." He thrust out his thick neck. "Nobody," he said flatly, "hass come back through this arbor at all."

By nine o'clock that night, terror had come to the Hotel Suchard.

Until then Monsieur Gant, the manager, had refrained from summoning the police. At first Monsieur Gant appeared to think that everybody was joking. He only began to gesticulate, and to run from room to room, when it became clear that Betty Weatherill was not to be found either in the hotel or in the grounds. If the testimony were to be believed—and neither Dermot nor Vanderver would retract one word—then Betty Weatherill had simply walked into the arbor, and there had vanished like a puff of smoke.

It was certain that she had not left the arbor by, say, getting out through the vines. The vines grew up from the ground in a matted tangle like a wire cage, so trained around their posts from floor to arch that it would be impossible to penetrate them without cutting. And nowhere were they disturbed in any way. There was not—as one romantic under-porter suggested—an underground passage out of the tunnel. It was equally certain that Betty could not have been hiding in the arbor when Dermot walked through it. There was no place there to hide in.

This became only too clear when the Chinese lanterns were lighted in the greenish tunnel, and Monsieur Gant stood on a stepladder to shake frantically at the vine-walls—with half the domestic staff twittering behind him. This was a family matter, in which everybody took part.

Alys Marchand, in fact, was the backstairs-heroine of the occasion. Alys was the plump waitress who had been sent to fetch fresh tea and sandwiches not fifteen minutes before Betty's disappearance, but who had not brought them back because of a disagreement with the cook as to what hours constituted feev-o'clock-tay.

Apart from Dermot, Alys had been the last person to see Betty Weatherill in the flesh. Alys had passed unscathed through the arbor. To Monsieur Gant she described, with a wealth of gesture, how she had taken the order for tea and sandwiches from Monsieur Dermot. She showed how she had picked up the big tray, whisking a cloth over its debris like a conjuror. A pink-cheeked brunette, very neat in her black frock and apron, she illustrated how she had walked back through the arbor towards the hotel.

Had she seen Dr. Vanderver on this occasion?

She had.

Where was he?

At the little table on the terrace. He was smoking a cigar, and sharpening a big horn-handled knife on a small whetstone block he carried in his pocket.

"That," interposed Vanderver, in excellent French, "is a damned lie."

It was very warm in the arbor, under the line of Chinese lanterns. Vanderver stood against the wall. He seemed less bovine when he spoke French. But a small bead of perspiration had appeared on his forehead, up by the large vein near the temple; and the expression of his eyes behind the thick spectacles turned Andrew Dermot cold.

"It is true as I tell you," shrieked Alys, turning round her dark eyes. "I told my sister Clothilde, and Gina and Odette too, when I went to the kitchen. He thrusts it into his pocket—quick, so!—when he sees me."

"There are many uses for knives," said Monsieur Gant, hastily and nervously. "At the same time, perhaps it would be as well to telephone the police. You are an advocate, Monsieur Dermot. You agree?"

Dermot did agree.

He had been keeping tight hold of his nerves. In fact, he found the cold reason of his profession returning to him; and it was he who directed matters. Instead of bringing back the nightmare, this practical situation steadied him. He saw the issue clearly now. It became even more clear when they arrived, amid a squad of plainclothes men, none other than Monsieur Lespinasse, the *juge d'instruction.*

After examining the arbor, M. Lespinasse faced them all in the manager's office. He was a long, lean, melancholy man with hollow cheeks, and the Legion of Honor in his buttonhole. He had hard uncomfortable eyes, which stared down at them.

"You understand," said Lespinasse, "we appear to have here a miracle. Now I am a realist. I do not believe in miracles."

"That is good," said Dermot grimly, in his careful French. "You have perhaps formed a theory?"

"A certainty," said Lespinasse.

The hard uncomfortable eyes turned on Dermot.

"From our examination," said Lespinasse, "it is certain that Mlle. Weatherill did not leave the arbor by any secret means. You, monsieur, tell one story." He looked at Vanderver. "You, monsieur, tell another." He looked back at Dermot. "It is therefore evident that one of you must be telling a lie."

Vanderver protested at this.

"I remind you," Vanderver growled, with a significant look, "that it will be unwise for you to make mistakes. As an acting representative of His Majesty the King of Sylvania, I enjoy immunities. I enjoy privileges—"

"Diplomatic privileges," said Monsieur Lespinasse. "That is no concern of mine. My concern is that you do not break the civil law."

"I have broken no law!" said Vanderver, purple in the face. "I have told no lie!"

The *juge d'instruction* held up his hand.

"And I tell you in return," he said sharply, "that either your story or Monsieur Dermot's must be untrue. Either the young lady never went into the arbor, in which case Monsieur Dermot is telling a falsehood. Or else she did go in, and for some reason you choose to deny that you saw her come out. In which case—" Again he held up his hand. "It is only fair to warn you, Dr. Vanderver, that Miss Weatherill told me you might try to kill her."

They could hear a clock ticking in the overcrowded room.

"Kill?" said Vanderver.

"That is what I said."

"But I did not know her!"

"Evidently she knew you," answered M. Lespinasse. His sallow face was alive with bitterness; he fingered the rosette in his buttonhole. Then he took a step forward. "Miss Weatherill several times came to me at the prefecture of police. She told me of your— murderous activities in the past. I did not choose to believe her.

It was too much of a responsibility. Responsibility! Now this happens, and I must take the responsibility for it at least. One more question, if you please. What have you to say to the maid's story of the horn-handled knife?"

Vanderver's voice was hoarse. "I never owned such a knife. I never saw one. I call you a son of—"

"It will not be necessary to finish," said the *juge d'instruction*. "On the contrary, we shall finish." He snapped his fingers, and one of the plain-clothes men brought into the room an object wrapped in a newspaper.

"Our search of the arbor," continued M. Lespinasse, "was perhaps more thorough than that of Monsieur Gant. This was found buried in the sand floor only a few feet away from where monsieur was sitting."

There were more than damp stains of sand on the bright, wafer-thin blade in the newspaper; there were others. Monsieur Lespinasse pointed to them.

"Human blood," he said.

At eleven o'clock Andrew Dermot was able to get out of the room.

They told him afterwards that he had made an admirable witness; that his replies had been calm, curt, and to the point; and that he had even given sound advice on details of legal procedure, contrasting those of England with those of the present country.

He did not remember this. He knew only that he must get out into the air and stop himself from thinking of Betty.

He stood on the front terrace of the hotel, as far removed as possible from the arbor in whose floor the knife had been buried. Half a mile away the lights of the principal street in the town, the Promenade des Français, twinkled with deathly pallor. A cool wind swept the terrace.

They took Vanderver down the front steps and bundled him into a car. There was a chain round Vanderver's wrists; his legs shook so that they had to push him up into the car. The car roared away, with a puff of smoke from the exhaust—carbon monoxide, which meant death—and only the *juge d'instruction* remained behind searching Vanderver's room for some clue as to why a sudden, meaningless murder had been done at dusk beside a commonplace hotel.

Andrew Dermot put his hands to his temples, pressing hard.

Well, that was that.

He sat down on the terrace. The little round tables had red tops, and the color did not please him, but he remained. He ordered brandy, which he could not taste. The brandy was brought to him by the same under-porter who had suggested an underground passage in the arbor, and who, agog, seemed to want to entertain him with speculations about motives for murder. Dermot chased him away.

But if Betty had to go—"go" was hardly the word for that— where was the sense in it? Why? Why? Vanderver was presumably not a homicidal maniac. Besides, all Dermot's legal instincts were bewildered by so clumsy a crime. If Vanderver were guilty, why had he from the first persisted in that unnecessary lie of saying Betty had never come out of the arbor? Why hadn't he simply faded away, never professing to have seen anything at all? Why thrust himself at that entrance as though determined to ensure suspicion for himself?

What Dermot had not permitted himself to wonder was where Betty herself might be.

But suppose Vanderver had been telling the truth?

Nonsense! Vanderver could not be telling the truth. People do not vanish like soap-bubbles out of guarded tunnels.

Presently they would be turning out the lights here on this windy, deserted terrace. The Hotel Suchard was ready, in any case, to close its doors for the winter; it would close its doors very early tonight. Behind him, in lighted windows, glowed the lounge, the smoking-room, the dining-room where he had first seen Betty. The head porter, his footsteps rapping on hardwood, darkened first the dining-room and then the lounge. Dermot would have to go upstairs to his room and try to sleep.

Getting to his feet, he walked through the thick-carpeted hall. But he could not help it. He must have one more look at the arbor.

It was a veritable tunnel now: a black shape inside which, for twenty yards, Chinese lanterns glowed against the roof. The sand was torn where the knife had been dug out. Near that patch two shovels had been propped against the wall in readiness for deeper excavations next morning. It was when he noted those preparations, and realized what they meant, that Dermot's mind turned black; he had reached his lowest depth.

He was so obsessed by it that he did not, at first, hear footfalls on the tiled terrace. He turned round. Two persons had come out to join him—but they came by different windows; and they stopped short and stared at each other as much as they stared at him.

One of these persons was M. Lespinasse, the *juge d'instruction*.

The other was Betty Weatherill.

"And now, mademoiselle," roared Lespinasse, "perhaps you will be good enough to explain the meaning of this ridiculous and indefensible trick?"

M. Lespinasse, his cheek-bones even more formidable, was carrying a briefcase and a valise. He let both fall to the floor.

"I had to do it," said Betty, addressing Dermot. "I *had* to do it, my dear."

She was not smiling at him. Dermot felt that presently, in the sheer relief of nerves, they would both be shouting with laughter. At the moment he only knew that she was there, and that he could touch her.

"One moment," said Lespinasse, coldly interrupting what was going on. "You do well, Monsieur Dermot, to demand an explanation—"

"But I don't. So long as she's—"

"—of this affair." The *juge d'instruction* raised his voice. "I can now tell you, in fact I came downstairs to tell you, *how* Miss Weatherill played this trick. What I do not know is why she did it."

Betty whirled round. "You know how?"

"I know, mademoiselle," snapped the other, "that you planned this foolishness and carried it out with the assistance of Alys Marchand, who deserves a formidable stroke of the boot behind for her part in the affair. When I found Alys ten minutes ago capering round her room waving a packet of thousand-franc notes, her behavior seemed to call for some explanation." He looked grim. "Alys was very shortly persuaded to give one."

Then he turned to Dermot.

"Let me indicate what happened, and you shall confirm it! Miss Weatherill asked you to meet her here, even specifying the table you were to occupy, and said she would arrive after tea?"

"Yes," said Dermot.

"At half-past five she came through the arbor—first making certain that Dr. Vanderver was on the terrace in the place he always occupied, every day, to smoke a cigar at that hour?"

"I—yes."

"Miss Weatherill was easily persuaded to have a fresh cup of tea?"

"Well, I asked her to."

"The waitress, Alys, was then pottering round for no apparent reason among otherwise deserted tables?"

"She was."

"You gave the order to Alys," said Monsieur Lespinasse grimly.

"She picked up your tray—a big tray—whisking over it a large cloth to cover the dishes? Just as we later saw her do?"

"I admit it."

"Alys then walked away from you through the arbor. As she did so," leered Lespinasse, so intent that he made a face, "Miss Weatherill distracted your attention by getting a light for her cigarette. And kept your attention fixed on herself by dropping the cigarette, and pretending an agitation she did not feel."

Dermot gave a quick look at Betty. Whatever else this might be, it was not a hoax or a joke. Betty's face was white.

"Miss Weatherill held your attention," said Lespinasse, "so that Alys could slip back out of the arbor unnoticed. *Alys did not really go through the arbor at all!* Carrying the tray, she merely darted round the side of the arbor and returned unseen to the hotel by another way.

"Miss Weatherill was then ready to play the rest of the comedy. 'Discovering' the loss of her compact, *she* enters the arbor. Halfway up, in the darkness, is lying a stage-property these two have already left there. This is another tray: like the first, and covered with a cloth. But this cloth does not cover dishes. It covers—" Monsieur Lespinasse broke off.

He looked flustered and dishevelled, but in his wicked eye there was a gleam of admiration.

"Monsieur Dermot, I tell you a psychological truth. The one person in this world whose features nobody can remember are those of a waitress. You see her at close range; yet you do not see her. Should you doubt this, the next time in your abominable London you go into a Lyons or an A.B.C., try calling for your bill in a hurry and see if you can identify the particular young lady who served you with a cup of tea. I know it. So did Miss Weatherill.

"She was already wearing a thin black frock under her white one. The tray in the arbor contained the other properties by which a blonde is changed into a brunette, white stockings and shoes change to black, a tanned complexion is heightened to a vivid ruddiness. It was the clumsiest possible disguise because it needed to be no more. Dr. Vanderver never glanced twice at the black-clad figure in cap and apron who walked out of the arbor carrying a tray. He saw no black wig; he saw no false complexion; he saw nothing. In his mind there registered, 'waitress-has-passed': no more. Thus Miss Weatherill, inexpertly got up as Alys, passed safely through the dense shadow which the arbor casts on the terrace—carrying before her the tray whose cloth neatly hid the discarded white dress, stockings, and shoes."

The *juge d'instruction* drew a deep, whistling breath.

"Very well!" he said. "But what I wish to know is: why?"

"You don't see it even yet?" asked Betty.

"My deepest apologies," said Lespinasse, "if I am dense. But I do not see it. You cannot have liked cutting yourself so that you might get real blood to put on the knife you buried. But why? How does all this nonsense help us, when Dr. Vanderver has committed no crime?"

"Because he's Embassy," answered Betty simply.

"Mademoiselle?"

"He has diplomatic immunity," said Betty. "The government can't search him; can't even touch him. And so, you see, I had to get him arrested by the *civil* authorities so that his papers could be searched."

She turned to Dermot.

"Derry, I'm sorry," she went on. "That is, I'm sorry I'm not quite the candid-camera schoolmistress burbling to high heaven that I pretended to be. But I want to be just that. I want to enjoy myself. For the first time in all my life, I've enjoyed myself in the last month. What I mean is: I want to be with you, that's all. So, now that I'm chucking the beastly job—"

Monsieur Lespinasse swore softly. After remaining rigid for a moment, he picked up the briefcase and the valise he had dropped. Both were in green leather stamped in gold with the royal arms of Sylvania.

"—and of course," Betty was saying almost wildly, "the fellow's name wasn't 'Dr. Vanderver,' and he's no more a neutral than I am. Only he'd got that job on forged credentials, and he was safe. So I had to keep telling the *juge d'instruction* I suspected him of being a murderer. His real name is Karl Heinrich von Arnheim; and when Sir George—you know to whom I refer, Monsieur Lespinasse—asked me to go after him—"

Monsieur Lespinasse could not break the lock of the briefcase. So he opened a wicked-looking knife of his own to slit the leather; and so he found the secret.

"The English," he said, "are not bad." He waved the knife, which glittered against the light from the windows. "Dr. Vanderver will not, I think, leave the police station after all." He swept Betty Weatherill a profound bow. "The complete plans," he added, "of the underground fortifications whose fall would break the whole line of defense along this front."

The Black Cabinet

As the Emperor's closed carriage swung toward the private entrance at the Opera, with the gentlemen's carriages ahead and the white horses of the Imperial Guard clattering behind, three bombs were thrown from the direction of the Opera steps.

And, only a minute before, a small nine-year-old girl in the crowd had been almost mutinous.

She was too grownup, Nina thought, to be lifted up in *maman's* arms as though she were four years old or even six. True, the fusty-smelling coats and tall hats of the men, even the bonnets and crinolines of the women, made so high a black hedge that Nina could see little except the gas jets illuminating the façade of the Opera and the bright lamps of the Parisian street. But it was warm down here: warm, at least, for a night in mid-January of 1858.

Then up Nina went, on the arm of *maman*. Already they could hear in the distance the measured applause—the slow, steady clap-clap of hands, as at a play—and a ragged cheer as the procession approached.

But Nina did not even know what it was, or why they were here.

"Mother, I . . ." she began in French.

Maman's bonnet, lined with ruffles, was so long-sided that Nina could not see her mother's face until it was turned around. Then *maman's* dark Italian eyes, always so kindly, took on a glassy bulging glare of hatred and triumph as she pressed her lips against Nina's long curls; bright brown curls, like the hair of Nina's American father.

102

"Look well!" whispered the handsome Signora Maddalena Bennett, in the Italian language. "At last you will see the death of the devil."

And Nina understood. She too hated, as she had been taught to hate, without knowing why. She had been schooled not to sob or tremble. Yet tears welled up in her eyes, because Nina was sick with fear. In one of those carriages must be Napoleon the Third, Emperor of the French.

Clop-clop, clop-clop moved the horses; slowly, but ever nearer the carpet of white sand spread in front and at the side of the Opera. Then, suddenly, Signora Bennett's whole expression changed. She had never dreamed that the murderers—Orsini and his conspirators—would hold their hands so long, or might throw bombs from the very side or steps of the Opera itself.

"No!" she shrieked aloud.

Holding the child closely, Signora Bennett flung the side of her fur pelisse over Nina's head and dropped down into the half-frozen mud among the spectators. Just as she fell, a black object flew over the heads of the crowd, high-sailing against gas lamps.

Through a crack between the fur pelisse and maman's fashionable deep-bosomed gown with the steel buttons, Nina saw the edge of a white flash. Though they were protected, the first explosion seemed to crush rather that crash, driving steel needles through her eardrums. There were two more explosions, at seconds' intervals. But the street went dark at the first crash, blinding the gas lamps, setting the air a-sing with flying glass from lamps or windows. Nina's scream was lost amid other screams.

Afterward the small girl felt little or nothing.

A curtain of nightmare, now called shock, wrapped soothingly round Nina's mind and nerves. She looked without surprise, or with very little surprise, at anything she saw. Though her mother, also unhurt, still crouched and breathed heavily, Nina stood up on shaky legs.

Most of the black hedge of tall shiny hats had fallen away. It lay motionless, or tried to crawl across bloodied white sand. And, as Nina turned sideways, she saw the Emperor's state coach near the foot of the steps.

"Sire! Sire!" she heard military voices shouting, amid other shouts. And, above it, the bellow of a military policeman: "Sire!"

The great closed carriage was at a standstill. Stabbed with blast and steel splinters and needles of glass, it had toppled partly toward Nina but remained intact except for its windows. Also, by some miracle, one great gold-bound carriage lantern was still burning on this side.

Before the officers of the Emperor's bodyguard could reach the handle of the coach door, the door opened. There emerged a stately-looking man, plump rather than stout, who jumped to the coach step and thence to the ground.

The carriage lamp gleamed on gold epaulets against a blue coat, and white trousers. His (apparently) steady hand was just putting back on his head the overdecorated cocked hat he wore fore-and-aft. Nina knew, if only from pictures, that he was the Emperor. Though he might be sallow-faced and growing puffy under the eyes, yet between his heavy black moustaches and fox-brush of imperial beard there appeared the edge of a cool smile.

"He is not hurt, the Emperor! Louis Napoleon is unhurt!"

"Long live the Emperor!"

Gravely the sallow-faced man handed down from the carriage a pretty, bad-tempered lady, her countenance as white as her long pearl earrings; she must be the Empress Eugénie. Officers, their uniform coats torn and their faces slashed, whipped out sabers in salute.

"Long live the Empress!"

"And the Emperor! And the Emperor!"

A thick, low rattle of drums ran urgently along the line. Foot-soldiers, dark silhouettes, flowed across and stood up at present-arms, so that the Emperor might not see fallen men with half faces or women carrying bomb splinters where they might have carried children. Around that wrecked carriage, with its two dead horses, lay one hundred and fifty persons, dead or wounded.

The Emperor smiled broadly, concealing agitation.

For the first time genuine hatred, a hatred of what she saw for herself, entered into Nina Bennett and never left her. It made her small body squirm, choking back her voice. It may have been due partly to the teaching of her mother's friends of Young Italy, of the *Carbonari*, who derisively called Napoleon the Third "the sick parrot" when they did not call him devil. But now it was Nina's own hatred.

She could not have explained what had happened, even now. Though she had heard something of bombs, she did not even think of bombs—or of the men who had thrown them. Nina felt only that a white lightning bolt had struck down beside her, hurting, *hurting* these people and perhaps even making them die as her own father had died a year ago in Naples.

Yet the yellow-faced Emperor, with his black moustaches and imperial, had taken no scathe. He stood there and (to Nina) smiled hatefully. He had caused this. It was his fault. His!

Instinctively, amid the reek and the drum-beating, Nina cried out in English, the language her father had taught her, and which she spoke far better than French or even Italian.

"Sick parrot!" the small lungs screeched, the words lost. "Devil! Usurper!"

And then her mother enfolded her, feeling over her for wounds and whispering furiously.

"Be silent, my child! Not another word, I tell thee!"

Gathering up Nina under her fur pelisse, and adding indignity to hysteria, *maman* fought and butted her way out of the crowd with such fury that suspicious eyes turned. Up in front of them loomed a military policeman, his immense cocked hat worn sideways.

"The child!" cried Signora Bennett, clutching Nina with true stage effect, and tragically raised dark eyes to a dark muffled sky. "The child," she lied, "is injured!"

"Pass, madame," gruffly. "Regret."

Though the distance was not great, it took them almost an hour in the crowds to reach their fine furnished lodgings in the rue de Rivoli. There waited Aunt Maria, also Italian and maman's maid-companion, fiercely twisting the point of a knife into a rosewood table as she awaited news. Afterward Nina could remember little except a bumping of portmanteaux and a horrible seasickness.

For Signora Bennett, Nina, and Aunt Maria left Paris next day. They had long been safe in England when two of the bomb-assassins—Orsini and Pieri—dropped on the plank and looked out through the everlasting window of the guillotine.

And that had been just over ten years ago.

So reflected Miss Nina Bennett, at the very mature age of nineteen, on the warm evening early in July which was the third evening after her return to Paris. Nobody could have denied that she was beautiful. But all those years in England had made her even more reserved than the English, with a horror of elaborate gestures like those of her late mother.

Though the sky was still bright over the Place de la Concorde, Nina Bennett had told Aunt Maria to close the heavy striped curtains on the windows. Aunt Maria was very fat now. She had a faint moustache of vertical hairs, like a tiny portcullis between nose and mouth. As she waddled over to scrape shut the curtains and waddled back to her chair, wrath exuded from her like a bad perfume.

Nina sat at the dressing-table before a mirror edged in gold leaf.

Two gas jets, one in the wall on either side of the mirror, set up yellow flames in flattish glass dishes. They shone on Nina's pink-and-white complexion, her dark blue eyes, her bright brown hair parted in the middle and drawn across the ears to a soft, heavy pad along the nape of the neck. The evening gown of that year was cut just an inch and a half below each shoulder, curving down in lace across the breast; and Nina's gown was so dark a red that it seemed black except when the gaslight rippled or flashed.

Yet her intense composure gave Nina's beauty a chilly quality like marble. She sat motionless, unsmiling, her arms stretched out and hands lightly crossed on the dressing-table.

"No," she thought, "I am not unattractive." The thought, or so she imagined, gave her neither pleasure nor displeasure.

At her left on the dressing-table stood a great bouquet of yellow roses in a glass vase of water. Nina Bennett had bought them herself, as a part of her plan of death. In the dressing-table drawer lay the weapon of death.

"I have no heroics," she thought, looking at the reflection of her blue eyes. "I do not think of myself as Joan of Arc or Charlotte Corday. Though I may be insane, I do not believe so. But I will kill this puff-ball Emperor, who still mysteriously reigns over the French. I will kill him. I will kill him. I will kill him."

Her intensity was so great that she breathed faster, and faint color tinged her pink-and-white face. Suddenly, out of the darkling background in the mirror, she saw fat Aunt Maria, with gray-streaked hair and fishbone moustache, writhing and flapping with anger.

Aunt Maria's hoarse, harsh voice spoke in Italian.

"Now I wonder," sneered Aunt Maria, "why you must close the curtains, and dare not look on the beauty of Paris."

Nina hesitated before she replied, moistening her lips. Despite her flawless English speech and her tolerable French, she had half-forgotten her mother's Italian and must grope for it.

"You are at liberty," she said, "to wonder what you like."

Again Aunt Maria slapped the chair-arms and writhed, almost in tears. Never in her life could Nina believe that these gesticulations were real, as they were, and not mere theatricalism. Intensely she disliked them.

"Out there," panted Aunt Maria, "is the city of light, the city of pleasure. And who made it so? It was your loathed Louis Napoleon and Baron Haussmann, planning their wide boulevards and their lamps and greenery. If we now have the Wood of Boulogne, it is because Louis Napoleon loves trees."

Nina raised her brown eyebrows so slightly that they hardly seemed to move.

"Do you tell me," she asked, "the history of the sick parrot?"

The gas jets whistled thinly, in a shadowy room with black satin wall panels figured in gold. Gracefully, with a studied grace, Nina Bennett rose from the dressing-table, and turned around. The monstrous crinolines of the past decade had dwindled into smaller, more manageable hoopskirts which rustled with petticoats at each step. Glints of crimson darted along Nina's dark, close-fitting gown.

"Have you forgotten, Maria?" she asked, in a passionately repressed voice. "In these rooms, these very rooms, where we lived ten years ago? How you took a great knife, and stabbed a dozen times into the top of a rosewood table, when you heard Orsini had failed? Can you deny it?"

"Ah, blood of the Madonna!"

"Can you deny it?"

"I was younger; I was foolish!" The harsh voice rose in pleading. "See, now! This Emperor, in his youth, worshipped the memory of his uncle, the war-lord, the first Napoleon. The first Napoleon they exiled . . ."

"Yes," agreed Nina, "and kings crept out again to feel the sun."

Aunt Maria was galvanized. "That is a noble line; that is a heart-shaking line!"

"It is the late Mrs. Browning's. A trifle. No matter."

"Well! This young man—yes, yes, it is the way of all young men!—was also a republican; a lover of liberty; a member of the Carbonari itself. Once he promised us a united Italy. But he wavered, and more than a few of us tried to kill him. He wavers always; I say it! But has he not done much in these past few years to redeem his promise? Body of Bacchus! Has he not?"

Though Nina was not tall, she stood high above Maria in the chair and looked down at her indifferently. Nina's white shoulders rose very slightly in the dark red gown.

"Ah, God, your mother has taught you well!" cried Aunt Maria. "Too well!" She hesitated. "And yet, when she died six months ago, it did not seem to me that you were much affected."

"I did not weep or tear my hair, if that is what you mean."

"Unnatural! Pah, I spit! What do you care for Italy?"

"A little, perhaps. But I am an American, as was my father before me."

"So I have heard you say."

"And so I mean!" Nina drew a deep breath; the gown seemed to be constricting her heart as well as her flesh. "My father was of what they call New England, in the state of Massachusetts. His money, though my mother sneered, has kept us above poverty all these years." Her tone changed. "Poor Maria; do the closed curtains stifle you?"

Whereupon Nina, with the same grace in managing her hoop-skirt, went to the left-hand window and threw back the curtains. The fustiness of the room, the fustiness of the curtains, for some reason reminded her of men's greatcoats; Nina shivered without knowing why. Then she opened the curtains of the other window.

Outside, to the little wrought-iron balcony above the rue de Rivoli, was fastened a flagstaff at an oblique angle. From it floated the beloved flag, the flag of the Union, the stars and stripes little more than three years triumphant in bitter war.

"Now what patriotism," jeered Aunt Maria, "for a country you have never seen!"

"It is more than that," said Nina, wanting to laugh. "In a sense it protects us. Have you not heard . . . ?"

"Speak!"

"This is our Day of Independence, the Fourth of July."

"Mad! Mad! Mad!"

"I think not. His Majesty Napoleon the Third made a futile stupid attempt to establish an empire in Mexico. That did not please the States of America." Nina lifted her exquisite hands and dropped them. "But the traditional friendship of France and America has been renewed. This evening, less than an hour from now, your hypocritical Emperor drives in state to the Opera, for a French-American ball, with ceremonies. As his carriage crosses the Place de la Concorde into the rue Royale . . ."

Aunt Maria heaved her laundry-bag shape up out of the chair.

"Blood of the Madonna!" she screamed. "You do not mean this madwoman's gamble for tonight?"

"Oh, but I do." And for the first time Nina Bennett smiled.

There was a silence, while Nina stood with her back to the window, with the soft and magical sky glow competing with these harsh-singing gaslights. And Nina was uneasy.

She had expected Aunt Maria to stamp, to howl, even possibly to shout from the window for help. But the aging woman only fell back into the chair, not speaking. Tears flowed out of her eyes, tears running down grotesquely past her nose and the hair-spikes of her moustache. Nina Bennett spoke sharply.

"Come, Aunt Maria. This is ridiculous! Why should you weep?"

"Because you are beautiful," Aunt Maria said simply.

There was a silence.

"Well! I—I thank you, Maria. Still . . . !"

"Oh, your plan is good." Aunt Maria turned her streaming eyes toward the great bouquet of yellow roses on the dressing-table, and the drawer which held the weapon. "No doubt you will kill him, my dear. Then you will go to the guillotine, in bare feet and with a black veil over your head, because to kill the Emperor is an act of parricide. You will have had no life, none! No laughter. No affection. No love of men."

Nina's face had gone white. For some reason she retorted cruelly.

"And your own vast experience of love, dear Maria . . . ?"

"That too is ridiculous, eh? Oho, that is comic; yes? This to you!" Aunt Maria made the gesture. "For I have known love more than you think! And the good strong passion, and the heartache too. But you will not know it. You are poisoned; your veins are poisoned. If an honest lover bit your arm until the blood flowed, he would die. Ah, behold! You shrink in disgust like a cold Englishwoman!"

"No, good Maria. And Englishwomen are not cold, save perhaps in public. It is as stupid a legend as the legend that they are all fair-haired."

"Listen!" blurted Maria, dabbing at her eyes. "Do you know who poisoned you?"

"If you please, Maria . . . !"

"It was your own mother. Yes! Do you think she knew no man except your father? Body of Venus, she had enough lovers to fill a prison! I startled you? But, because she must dedicate you to her 'cause' of murder, she would turn you against men. How long she spoke to you, when you were thirteen or fourteen, in the accursed great cold house in London! Have I not seen you rush out of the drawing-room, crimson-faced, and your sainted mother laughing secretly?"

"I—I have thought of love," she said calmly. "I would love well, perhaps, if I did not hate. And now, Maria, it is time to fetch my jewel box; and set out my hat and cloak."

Aunt Maria paid no attention.

There was a wild shining of inspiration in her eyes, as though at last she had seen some way to turn this inflexible girl from a mad course. But the time was going, the time was going!

"Come, a test!" panted Aunt Maria. "Are you in truth as poisoned as I said?"

"Did you hear my command, Maria?"

"No! Listen! You remember three nights ago, the evening of the first day we came to Paris? How we returned from our walk, and the young man you met in the courtyard? Well, I saw your eyes kindle!" Aunt Maria cackled with mirth. "You an American? You are a Latin of the Latins! And this young man: was he French —or Italian?"

Nina Bennett grew rigid.

"You have strange fancies," she said. "I cannot remember this at all."

But she did remember it. As Nina turned around briefly to look out of the long window, where a faint breeze rippled the vivid colors of the stars and stripes, that whole brief scene was re-created in every detail.

As the courtesy-aunt said, it had been at about this time on the evening of July second. Aunt Maria had marched beside Nina as they returned from their walk. Even in this modern age, the most emancipated American or English girl would not have gone through such tree-bewitched streets, full of summer's breath and mirrors a-wink in cafés without a formidable chaperone.

The house in which they had taken furnished lodgings was unlike most of those in the same street. It was of an older day, patterned after a nobleman's *hôtel*. Through a smaller door in high-arched wooden doors you passed through a cool tunnel smelling of old stone, with the *concierge's* lodge on the right. Then you emerged into a green courtyard; it had galleries built around on three sides, and stone balustrades carved with faces. An outside staircase led up to each gallery. In the middle of the green, scented turf was a dead fountain.

As Aunt Maria creaked up the staircase, Nina followed her. Vaguely Nina had noticed a young man standing a little distance away, smoking a cigar and leaning on a gold-headed stick. But she paid little attention. In both hands, if only for practice's sake, she carried a large bouquet of red roses in which was hidden a small but heavy object, and two fingers of her right hand held the chains of her reticule. Though strung-up and alert, Nina was very tired.

Perhaps that was why the accident happened. When she had gone six steps up behind Aunt Maria, Nina's reticule—a heavy, flower-painted handbag—slipped through her fingers, bounced down the steps, and landed on the lowermost one.

"Ah, so-and-so!" exclaimed Aunt Maria, and wheeled around her moustache.

There was a flick in the air as the dark-complexioned young man flung away his cigar. He had suffered some injury to his left leg. But, so deft was his use of the stick, that he scarcely seemed to limp when he made haste. In an instant he was at the foot of the staircase.

The cane was laid down. With his left hand he swept off his high, glossy hat, and his right hand scooped up the reticule. His eyes strayed to Nina's ringless left hand.

"If you will permit me, mademoiselle . . . ?" he said.

The man, whether French or Italian, had a fine resonant voice, fashioning each French syllable clearly. His dark hair, parted on one side, was so thick that it rose up on the other side of the parting. A heavy moustache followed the line of his delicate upper lip. His somber dark clothes, though carelessly worn, were of fine quality.

Nina Bennett, who had turned around, looked down the stairs straight into his eyes. Nina, in a dress of dark purple taffeta and a boat-shaped hat with a flat plume, would have denied coldly that she was a romantic.

"But he is undeniably handsome," she was thinking, "and without oiliness or exaggeration. He has endured great suffering, by the whiteness of his face and the little gray in his hair. And yet his mockery of eye, as though he knew too much of women . . . !"

Abruptly Nina straightened up.

"I thank . . ." she began coldly; and then the worst happened.

Nina, still holding the bouquet of red roses, either by accident or nervousness, jerked her left wrist against the stair-balustrade. The roses seemed to spill apart. Out of their stems leaped a derringer, short of barrel but large of bore. It banged on the step, and clattered down to the lowermost one. Though it was loaded with wad, powder, and heavy ball, it did not explode; there was no percussion-cap on the firing-nipple.

Nina stood rigid with horror, like Aunt Maria. For a moment, in that shadowy green courtyard under the light of a pink sunset, it was as silent as though they stood in the Forest of Marly.

The young man looked strangely at the pistol, and suddenly jumped back as though he feared it might still go off. Then he smiled. After a swift glance at the lodge of the concierge, he dropped the reticule on top of the derringer, concealing it. He picked up both, advanced up the stairs, and gravely handed the fallen objects to Nina.

"Permit me, mademoiselle, to return your reticule and your—your protection against footpads. If I might suggest . . ."

"I thank you, monsieur. But it is not necessary to suggest."

"Alas, I have already done so," he said, and again looked her in the eyes. His French voice both pointed the double meaning, yet smilingly robbed the words of offense. Pressing the brim of his hat against the black broadcloth over his heart, he bowed slightly. "Until a re-meeting, mademoiselle!"

"Until a re- . . ." said Nina, and stopped. She had not meant to speak at all.

Whirling around her skirts, the roses and pistol and reticule like a mortifying weight in her arms, Nina marched up the stairs after Aunt Maria.

And this was the brief scene which returned in every detail to Nina Bennett, in the dark old room with the gas jets, during the moment when she looked out of the long window over the rue de Rivoli. She had only to concentrate, and it was gone forever. But she felt the pressure of Aunt Maria's eyes, wet and crafty, boring into her back; and anger rose again.

Turning around, Nina took four steps and stood over Aunt Maria in the chair.

"Why do you remind me of this?" Nina asked.

"Oh, then we were smitten!"

"Hardly." The voice was dry. But when Nina opened her blue eyes wide, Maria shrank back because they were maniacal and terrifying. "Do you imagine that some sordid affair of love would keep me back from the only cause I have for living?"

"This 'cause'!" sneered Aunt Maria. "I tell you, it is a cold warming-pan for a long night, instead of a husband. Away with it! With your looks and your money: body of Bacchus, you might wed any man you chose." Abruptly, amid her tears, the fat woman began to cackle again with laughter. "But not the young Italian of the courtyard, poor Nina! No, no! Not that one!"

"And why not?" demanded Nina.

"Listen, my child. Pay heed to an old conspirator like me! For I have seen them all. I know the ingratiating air, the cringing approach, the mark of the almost-gentleman . . ."

"How dare you!" Nina amazed herself by crying out. Then she controlled her voice. "You will allow me, please, to pass my own judgment on a gentleman."

"Oh, then we were not smitten! Oh, no!" cackled Aunt Maria. Then her laughter died. "Shall I tell you what this young man really is?"

"Well?"

"He is what the French call a *mouchard*. A police spy."

"You lie!" A pause. "In any event," Nina added casually, "it is of no importance. Since you disobey my order to fetch my hat and cloak and jewel box . . ."

"No, no, I will find them!" said Aunt Maria, and surged up out of the chair.

On creaking slippers she wheezed across to an immense dark wardrobe beside the door and opposite the windows. Opening one door of the wardrobe, she plucked out a waist-length cape of rich material in stripes of silver and wine-red.

"Well!" snorted Aunt Maria, examining the cape and giving no sign of furious thought. "You will go to kill the Emperor. I have promised not to interfere; good, I keep my promise! But it will be sad for you, hot-blood, when they arrest you—as they will, mark it!—before you have fired the shot."

Nina's gaze had gone to the grandfather clock, near the alcove which housed the big curtained bed. The time—the time was running out. True, she still had many minutes. But there would be a crowd. She must be in place, the exact spot she had chosen, long before the Imperial procession went past.

Now the meaning of Maria's words stabbed into her brain for the first time.

"What did you say, fuss-budget?"

"Enough," muttered the fat woman darkly. "I said enough!"

"Come, good Maria. Is this another of your childish tricks to divert me?"

"Childish!" cried Aunt Maria, now in a real temper. "Was I your mother's companion for twenty years, or was I not? Do I know every dog's-tail of plotting, or do I not?"

"Of old and clumsy plotting, yes. But my device . . ."

"Faugh!" snorted Aunt Maria, past patience. "How do you think Louis Napoleon keeps so quiet his bright city, his toy? Ask the Prefect of Police, M. Pietri—yes, I said Pietri, not Pieri—but above all ask M. Lagrange, the chief of the political police! They buy more spies than the sand-grains at Dieppe! By my immortal soul, Lagrange will stir up a riot for the very joy of showing how quickly he can suppress it!"

Aunt Maria shook the cape. With her own version of a haughty shrug, she reached again into the wardrobe and drew out a very wide-brimmed velvet hat of the same dark red as Nina's gown.

"You don't believe an old woman, eh?" she taunted. "Good! For I have finished with you. But this I swear on the Cross: you have been betrayed."

"Lies and lies and lies! Betrayed by whom?"

"Why, by your young man down in the courtyard."

She was going dangerously far, to judge by Nina's eyes and breathing.

"Little stupid!" she continued to taunt. "Did you not observe how he started and jumped, when the pistol fell at his feet? He thought there might be a bullet for *him*. Did you not see how he looked with quickness towards the lodge of the *concierge*, who was watching? The *concierge*, who feeds the police with a spoon! You a plotter, when you gave your true name of Bennett? Pah! The name of your mother is a very passport to the Prefecture!"

Now Aunt Maria did not actually believe one word of what she had said about the young man. In fact, three nights ago she had scarcely noticed him except as a possible moustache-twisting sinner of the boulevards. But these ideas foamed into her brain; she could not stop; she must speak faster and faster.

For it seemed to her that there was a hesitation in Nina's eyes . . .

Nina moved slowly to the side of the dressing-table, still looking steadily at the other woman. Gaslight burnished the wings of Nina's soft brown hair. With her left hand she pulled open the drawer of the dressing-table, in which the derringer pistol lay fully loaded, and with a percussion-cap resting under the light pressure of its hammer.

"What do you do?" Aunt Maria screamed out. Then, abruptly glancing at the door and holding up cape and hat as though to call for silence, she added: "Listen!"

Outside the door, the only door in the room, was a drawing room with a polished hardwood floor unmuffled by any carpet. There was a sound. Both women heard the soft thump of the cane as the visitor slid forward a lame leg; then silence; then again the bump of the cane. Someone was slowly but steadily approaching the bedroom door. Both women knew who it was.

"My God!" thought the staggered Aunt Maria. "He really *is* a *mouchard* after all!"

A fist, not loudly, but firmly and with authority, knocked at the bedroom door.

Aunt Maria, terrified, backed away towards the bed alcove and held up cape and hat as though they might shield her.

If there had ever been any uncertainty in Nina's face, it was gone now. Her cold movements were swift but unhurried. From the vase she whipped the bouquet of yellow roses, squeezing the water from the stems and wrapping them in heavy tissue paper from the drawer. Gripping the stems in her left hand, she plucked out the pistol. There was a soft click as she drew back the hammer. She made an opening in the roses, hiding the derringer so that nothing should catch in the hammer when she snatched it out.

There would still be time to reload if she must dispose of an intruder first.

"Enter!" Nina calmly called in French. It was the language they spoke afterwards.

Their visitor, the man of the courtyard, came in and closed the door behind him. He was in full evening dress, partly covered by his ankle-length black cloak, which yet showed his white frilled shirtfront and a carelessly tied stock. In one white-gloved hand he held his hat, in the other his gold-headed stick.

Again Nina noted the delicacy of his white, handsome face, in contrast to the heavy dark hair and moustache. Even his figure was somewhat slight, though well-made.

"For this intrusion," he said in his fine voice, "I deeply apologize to mademoiselle; and, understood," bowing towards Aunt Maria, "to madame."

Nina's pink lips went back over fine teeth.

"Your best apology lies behind you." She nodded towards the door.

"Unfortunately, no." The stranger, at leisure, put down his hat and stick on a table at the left of the door. His dark eyes, with that odd life-in-death quality, grew strong with a fierce sincerity; and so did his voice. "For I presume to have an interest in you, mademoiselle."

"Who are you? What do you want?"

The stranger leaned his back against the door, seeming to lounge rather than lean, in a devil-may-care swagger which to Nina seemed vaguely familiar.

"Let us say that I am the detective Lecoq, in the admirable police-romances of M. Gaboriau. Lecoq is a real person, remember, as was the character D'Artagnan. Well! I am Lecoq."

Nina breathed a little faster. Her finger tightened round the trigger of the pistol.

"How did you enter by a locked front door?"

"Believe me, I have passed through more difficult doors than that. Stop!" His white-gloved hand went up to forestall her, and he smiled. "Let us suppose (I say merely let us suppose!) that

Mademoiselle Nina Bennett had intent to kill the Emperor of the French. I who speak to you, I also live in this house. I can put questions to a *concierge*."

"Did I not tell you?" screamed Aunt Maria, hiding her face behind cape and hat.

Neither of them looked at her.

"To any reader of the French journals, the name of your mother is well known. The nationality of your father," and he nodded toward the flag outside the window, his nostrils thin and bitter, "you too obviously display. However! If it be your intent to kill the Emperor, where would you go? Assuredly not far from here, or you would have been gone now."

("If you must kill this sly one here," Aunt Maria thought wildly, "kill him now! Shoot!")

"I think," continued the stranger, "you have chosen the corner of the rue Royale and the rue de Rivoli. Every journal in Paris will have told you, with exactness, the route and time of the procession. It is summer; there will be an open carriage, low-built. The Emperor, a fact well known, sits always on the right-hand side facing forward, the Empress on the left.

"How lovely . . ." His strong voice shook; he checked himself. "How innocent you will look, in your finery and jewels, chattering English and deliberately bad French, on the curbstone! The military, even the military police, will only smile when you walk out slowly toward the slow-moving carriage, and speak English as you offer—is it not so?—the bouquet of roses to the Empress Eugénie of Montijo."

("I was mad, I was mad!" mentally moaned Aunt Maria. "Let him take the damned pistol from her now!")

"Holding the bouquet in your left hand," he went on quietly, "you must lean partly across His Majesty. With your right hand you will take out an old-style single-shot pistol, and fire it at the

Emperor's head so closely that you cannot miss. Have I, M. Lecoq, correctly deduced your plan?"

Nina Bennett cast a swift glance at the clock.

Time, time, time! A while ago, when she had looked out of the window, far up to the right there had been a red sky over Neuilly beyond the top of the Champs Elysées. Now the whole sky was tinged with pink amid white and pale blue. It brightened the gaslights in that black-silk-paneled room, which might have been a symbol of espionage since the days of Savary and Napoleon the First.

"Are you the only one," Nina asked levelly, "who knows of this —this plan?"

"The only one, mademoiselle."

With a steady hand Nina took the derringer from among the roses, moving aside the yellow bouquet. It is a sober fact that the young man did not even notice it.

"And now," he said in that hypnotic voice, "I must tell you of my interest in you. It is very easy." He straightened up, his face whiter, and clenched his gloved fists. "You are Venus in the body of Diana; you are Galatea not yet kissed to true life. You are—I will not say the most beautiful woman I have ever met—but the most maddening and stimulating." Cynicism showed in his eyes. "And I have known so many women."

"How modest you are!" Nina cried furiously.

"I state a fact. But I tell you one of the reasons, my love, why I will not permit you to go from this room for at least half an hour."

Again Nina started, almost dropping the pistol.

From the street below, and from the open spaces beyond, there were cries and shouts. She heard the confused running of feet, seeming to come from every direction at once, which can conjure up a Paris crowd in one finger-snap. Very faintly, in the distance, she also heard the slow clop-clop of many horses in procession.

According to every newspaper, the procession to the Opera would be headed by the Imperial Band. The instruments of the band were clear rather than brassy; already they had begun with the swinging tune, "*Partant pour la Syrie*," which was the official song of Napoleon the Third.

> Setting out for Syria
> Young and brave Dunois . . .

There was still time. Nina Bennett's hand was as steady as a statue's.

"You call yourself a detective, M. Lecoq. But you are only a police spy. Now stand away from that door!"

"No, my dear," smiled the other, and folded his arms lazily.

"I will count to three . . ."

"Count to five thousand; I would hear your voice. What matter if you kill me? Most people," and his dark eyes seemed to wander out to the boulevards, "think me already dead. Put your hand in mine; let fools flourish pistols or knives."

"One!" said Nina, and thought she meant it.

The clop-clop of the procession, though still not loud, was drawing nearer. What sent a shiver through Nina's body was the tune into which the band changed, in honor of the French-American ball at the Opera. There were no words. There were only dreams and memories. Slow, somber, the great battle-hymn rolled out.

> Mine eyes have seen the glory of the coming of the Lord,
> He is trampling out the vintage where the grapes of wrath
> are stored. . . .

"In a moment," continued the visitor, unhearing, "I will come and take that pistol from you. It does not become you. But first hear what I have to say." His tone changed, fiercely. "This political assassination is more than wrong. It changes nothing. It is the act of an idiot. If I could make you understand . . ."

Abruptly he paused.

He, too, had heard the music, clear in the hush of evening. His face darkened. Had Aunt Maria been watching, she would have seen in his eyes the same maniacal glitter as in those of Nina Bennett. And he spoke the only words which could have ended his life.

"By God!" he snarled. "You might have been a human being, without your mother and your damned Yankee father!"

Nina pulled the trigger, firing straight for his heart at less than ten feet's distance. The percussion-cap flared into the bang of the explosion, amid heavy smoke. The stranger, flung back against the door, still stood upright and emerged through smoke.

She had missed the heart. But the pistol-ball, smashing ribs on the right of his chest, had torn open his right lung. And Nina knew that never, never in her life, could she have fired at the Emperor unless he had first uttered some maddening insult.

"I thank you, my dear," gravely said the stranger, pressing his reddening fingers to his chest, and white-faced at his own choked breathing. "Now be quick! Put that derringer into my hand; and I shall have time to say I did it myself."

Then another realization struck Nina.

"You've been speaking in English!" she cried in that language. "Ever since you said 'damned Yankee.' Are you English?"

"I am an American, my dear," he answered, drawing himself up and swallowing blood. "And at least no one can call me a police spy. My name," he added casually, "is John Wilkes Booth."

A SIR HENRY MERRIVALE
NOVELETTE

All in a Maze

When Tom Lockwood first saw her, she was running down the stairs in terror. Behind her stretched the great sweep of stairs up to the portico of St. Paul's; above, Paul's Dome almost shut out the gray spring sky. A pigeon fluttered its wings. But there were very few people to see what happened.

The girl glanced over her shoulder. She was still so badly frightened that Tom's first thought was instinctive: she might stumble and pitch headlong. So he ran towards her.

His next thought, born of his journalistic work, was the grotesqueness of this whole scene, as the bell boomed out the stroke of four: a very pretty girl, with dark hair and wide-spaced gray eyes, fleeing in blind panic from the House of God.

Then she did stumble.

Tom caught her before she fell, and lifted her up gently by the elbows.

"Steady does it, you know," he said, and smiled down at her. "There's nothing to be afraid of, really."

Instantly she recoiled; then she saw his expression, and hesitated. Tom Lockwood's own mother could not have called him handsome. But he had such an engaging and easy-going expression, especially in his smile, that almost any woman would have trusted him on sight—and would have been right.

"*Nothing* to be afraid of," he repeated.

"Isn't there?" the girl blurted out. "When last night, by some

127

miracle no one can understand, they try to kill me? And now, just now, a voice speaks where no voice could have spoken? And tells me again I am going to die?"

Taxis hooted up Ludgate Hill. A rather sinister-looking policeman stood at the left-hand side of St. Paul's churchyard. Tom had a topsy-turvy sense that he did not really hear the words she was speaking.

She spoke with passion, in a beautiful voice with—was it?—some very faint tinge of accent. Her hair really was black and shining, worn in a long bob; the gray eyes, their pupils dilated with fear, had long black lashes. Tom was so conscious of her physical presence that he hastily let go her elbows.

"You don't believe me!" she cried. "Very well! I must go."

"No! Wait!"

The girl hesitated, looking at the pavement.

And Tom Lockwood was inspired almost to eloquence.

"You're alone," he said. "Oh, there may have been people with you in the Cathedral! But you're alone in yourself; you feel lost; you don't trust anybody. Will you trust a perfect stranger, if I tell you I only want to help you?"

To his intense embarrassment, tears came into her eyes.

"What you need—" he began. It was on the tip of his tongue to say "a couple of whiskies," but, in his present exalted mood, he decided this was unromantic. "Across the road," he said, "there's a tea shop of sorts. What you need is to drink tea and tell me your troubles. After all, hang it, I'm a reasonably respectable bloke! You see that policeman over there?"

"Yes?"

"*He* knows me," said Tom. "No, no, not because I'm an old lag just out of jail! As a matter of fact, I'm a crime reporter for the *Daily Record*. Here's my press-card."

"You are journalist?"

Her eyes flashed up; she pronounced the word almost as *journaliste*.

"Not where you are concerned. Please believe that! And you—are you by any chance French?"

"I am English," she retorted proudly, and drew herself up to her full height of five feet one. "Ah, bah! I am named Jenny. Jenny Holden. That is English enough, surely?"

"Of course. And I'm Tom Lockwood."

"But, you see," Jenny continued, "I have lived most of my life in France. When they brought me here for a visit, things seemed all funny but very nice, until—"

Jenny glanced back over her shoulder. Fear struck again, as though some terrifying presence lurked inside the Cathedral.

"Mr. Lockwood," she said, "of course I will go with you. And we need not be introduced by a policeman." Then her passionate voice rose. "But let us hurry, hurry, hurry!"

They dodged across through the skittish traffic to the tea shop at the corner of Paternoster Row. They passed the policeman in question, who seemed to fascinate Jenny. He was one of the Old Brigade: bulky and almost seven feet tall, just what any foreign visitor would expect to see.

Tom waved at him by way of greeting. The law saluted gravely but, when Jenny's head turned away, gave her companion a wink of such outrageous knowingness that Tom's ears went red.

At the door of the tea shop, however, Tom hesitated and turned round.

"Stop a bit! Was there somebody with you at St. Paul's?"

"Yes, yes! My Aunt Hester and my Cousin Margot."

"*They* didn't frighten you?"

"No, of course not!" Jenny's lips became mutinous. "I do not like my Aunt Hester. She behaves like a duchess, with a lorgnette, and you can hear her talking all over a restaurant. You know what I mean?"

"Bitterly well."

"My Cousin Margot, she is young and I like her. But I wish to get away from them. Please!"

"Right," said Tom, opening the door. "In you go."

He allowed the door to close very briefly behind her so that she should not hear him when his voice carried clearly across to the policeman.

"Dawson! You haven't seen us. Understand?"

The law did. His wink was more portentous than ever.

In the tea shop, more properly a tea bar, two girls chattered and banged tins behind the counter. But the place was deserted, including the two booths at the back. When the newcomers sat opposite each other in the farther booth, over thick mugs of a beverage which was at least hot, Jenny's terror was decreasing. She accepted a cigarette, had it lighted for her, and hesitated. Then she burst out: "You see, it is so difficult to say! I don't wish you to think I am silly, or have fancies, or am off my head. That is what *they* think."

" 'They'?"

"Aunt Hester. And others."

"Aunt Hester," said Tom, "shall be hung out on the clothes-line, preferably upside down, at the first opportunity. Meanwhile . . ."

He broke off, because Jenny bubbled with that laughter he came to know so well.

"You are nice!" she declared, like a magistrate imposing sentence. "Oh, how it is pleasant to meet people who make you laugh! Instead of—"

Jenny stopped, and disquiet settled on her again.

"It is silly," she insisted, "but I must say it. Can you explain miracles?"

"No. But I know a man who can. Did you ever hear of Sir Henry Merrivale?"

"Sir Henry *Merrivale*?"

"Yes."

"But he is awful!" cried Jenny. "He is fat and bald, and he swear and carry on and throw people out of windows."

"He is not, perhaps," Tom admitted, "quite the ladies' man he thinks he is. But he can explain miracles, Jenny. That's his purpose in life nowadays."

"You mean this?"

"Yes, I mean it."

"Then I had better explain from the beginning. My name—"

"I know your name," said Tom, looking at the table. "I am likely to remember it for a very long time."

There was a pause, while both of them hastily swallowed tea.

"Well!" said Jenny. "My father and mother went to live in France, at Cannes, before I was born. What with the war, and everything else, I had never been to England. My mother died during the war. My father died two years ago. My guardian is my father's old friend Général de Senneville. And I am now twenty-five: in France, I am what you would call in England an old maid."

"Are you, now?" breathed Tom, almost with awe. "Oh, crikey! Have you ever seen yourself in a mirror?"

Jenny looked at him, and then went on very quickly.

"It was always my father's wish I should come to England. I should see all the sights like any tourist: Westminster Abbey, the Tower of London, St. Paul's—"

"Steady, now!"

"Yes, I am steady. Général de Senneville, my guardian, said this plan was a good one, and did much honor to everyone. So he sent me, in charge of my Aunt Hester, just before I get married."

"Before you—!" Tom blurted out, and then stopped.

Jenny's face went pink. Tom, in the act of lighting a cigarette for himself, held the match for so long that it burned his fingers. He cursed, dropped both match and cigarette into the mug of tea; then, to hide his expression, he shoved the mug of tea down on the floor under the seat.

"But what else could I do?" Jenny asked defensively. "It was arranged many years ago, between my father and the général. At twenty-five, and an old maid, surely that was best?"

The damage had been done. They could not look at each other's eyes.

"And who's the bloke you're marrying?" he asked casually.

"Armand de Senneville. The général's son."

"Do you love him?"

All Jenny's English feelings warred with her strict French up-bringing.

"But you are not practical!" she exclaimed, the more vehemently because her feelings won every time. "An arranged marriage always turns out best, as the général says. It is understood that I do not love Armand, and Armand does not love me. I marry him because —well! it must be done, at twenty-five. He marries me because he wishes to obtain my dowry, which is very large."

"*Does he, by God!*"

"How dare you!"

"These old French customs." Tom folded his arms moodily. "You hear about 'em, you know they exist, but they're still hard to believe. What about this Armand de Senneville? He has oily black hair, I suppose, and sidewhiskers down his cheeks?"

"You must not speak so of my fiancé, and you know it!"

"All right, all right!"

"He has dark hair, yes, but none of the rest of it. He is charming. Also, he is one of the best businessmen in France. Armand is only thirty-five, but already he owns three newspapers, two in Paris and one in Bordeaux."

"Whereas I . . ."

"You said?"

"Nothing. He's with you, I suppose?"

"No, no! He was bitterly opposed to this holiday. He could not get away from business; he speaks no English and does not like the English. He has to consent, because his father wishes it. But he warns Aunt Hester to keep a sharp eye on me, in case I should be silly and fall in love with some dull, stupid Englishman—"

Abruptly Jenny paused. Her own cigarette, unnoticed, was burning her fingers; she threw it on the floor.

Tom looked straight at her.

"Which you might do, mightn't you?"

"No! Never! Besides, Aunt Hester and the de Sennevilles would never let me."

While Stella and Dolly clattered tins and banged cups behind the counter of a prosaic tea bar, Tom Lockwood took a great and secret and mighty resolve. But he did not show it in his brisk tone.

"Now, then! Let's get down to cases. What has frightened you so much?"

"Last night," answered Jenny, "someone tried to kill me. Someone turned on the tap of the gas heater in my bedroom. It was impossible for this to be done, because all the doors and windows were locked on the inside. But it was done. Already I had a note saying I was going to die."

Jenny's eyes seemed to turn inwards.

"By good luck, they save me. But I don't wish to speak of last night! This morning I am very—sick is not a nice word, is it?—no! I am ill. But Aunt Hester said this was nonsense, and it would revive me to go sightseeing again. That is why we went to St. Paul's. Do you know St. Paul's?"

"I'm afraid I haven't even been inside the place for a long time."

"It happened," said Jenny, "in the whispering gallery."

Whispering gallery.

The eerie sibilance tapped against the nerves even in this commonplace tea bar, with traffic rushing outside.

"You climb up stairs," said Jenny. "Spiral stairs. Stairs and stairs, until you are breathless and think you will never get to the top. Then there is a tiny little door, and you go out into the gallery."

Then Tom remembered—how vividly this whispering gallery had impressed him. It was dizzily high up, just under the curve of the dome: circular, some two hundred feet across, and with only an iron railing to keep you from pitching down interminably to the acres of folding chairs on the ground floor below.

Noises struck in with brittle sharpness. Gray light filtered in on the tall marble statues of saints round the vast circle. It was solemn, and it was lonely. Only one verger, black-clad, stood guard there.

More than ever Tom was conscious of Jenny's presence, of her parted lips and quick breathing.

"I am not a coward," she insisted. "But I did not like this place. If you sit on the stone bench round the wall, and someone—even two hundred feet away—whispers near the wall, that whisper comes round in a soft little gurgly voice out of nowhere.

"Please attend to me!" Jenny added, with deep sincerity. "I was not well—I admit it. But I was not unbalanced either. Ever since I have received that first note saying I would die, I have watch everyone. I trust nobody—you were right. But I trust you. And, on my oath, this happened as I tell it.

"There were only five persons in all that dusky gallery. You could see. My Aunt Hester and my Cousin Margot. A fat red-faced countryman who is come to see the sights with a packet of sandwiches and a thermos flask of tea. The verger, in a dark robe, who tells you about the gallery.

"That is all!

"First the verger showed us how the whispering gallery is worked. He leans against the wall to the left—you do not even have to be against the wall. He says something that we, on the right of the door, hardly hear at all. But it goes slipping and sliding and horrible round the dome. Something about 'This Cathedral, begun by Sir Christopher Wren—' and it jumps up in your ear from the other side.

"After that we separated, but only a little. I was nervous—yes, I admit that too! I sat down on the stone bench, all prim. Aunt

Hester and Margot went to the railing round the open space, and looked over. Margot giggles and says, 'Mama, would it not be dreadful if I jumped over?'

"Meanwhile, the fat countryman has sat down fifty feet away from me. Calmly he opens the grease-proof paper and takes out a sandwich. He pours out tea from the thermos into the cup; he is taking a deep drink when the verger, who is outraged at sandwiches in St. Paul's, rushes towards him from ten feet away.

"Mr. Lockwood, I know what I saw! The countryman could not have spoken; he is really and truly gulping down tea. The verger could not have spoken—I could see his mouth—and anyway he is too far away from the wall. As for Aunt Hester or Margot, that is nonsense! And, anyway, they are much too far away from the wall, and leaning over the railing.

"But someone spoke in my ear just then.

"It was in English, and horrible. It said: 'I failed the first time, Jennifer. But I shall not fail the second time.' And it gloated. *And there was nobody there!*"

Jenny paused.

With all the nervousness of the past days, there were shadows under her eyes, and she was more than pale. But a passion of appeal met Tom across the table.

"No, I did not say anything!" she told him. "If I had, Aunt Hester would only say I was imagining things. Just as she said I was imagining things last night, and must have turned on the gas-tap myself, because the room was all locked up inside.

"No, no, no! I jumped up and ran out. I ran down those stairs so fast no one could have caught me. I did not know where I was going or what I should do. If I prayed anything, I think I prayed to meet . . ."

"To meet whom?" prompted Tom.

"Well! To meet someone like you."

After saying this, defiantly, Jenny drank stone-cold tea.

"But what am I to do?" she demanded, with tears on her eye-lashes. "I know Aunt Hester means me no harm—how could she? But I can't face her—I won't! Where am I to go?"

"I will tell you exactly," said Tom, reaching across and taking her hands. "You are going with me to see old H.M., otherwise Sir Henry Merrivale, at an office which nowadays is humorously called The Ministry of Miracles. Afterwards—"

Bang!

The door of the tea bar flew open with a crash which half shattered its glass panel. Tom, sitting with his back to the door, first craned round and then leaped to his feet.

Outside the door, but not yet looking into the tea bar, stood an imperious and stately lady who was addressing someone beyond her.

"I am well acquainted, constable," she was saying, "with Sir Richard Tringham, the Commissioner of Police. Your deliberate falsehoods will not help you when I report you to him personally. You have denied you saw any young lady run down the steps of the Cathedral. You have denied she met a young man in sports coat and gray flannels. Finally, you have denied they went into any of the shops or other disgusting places along here. Is this so, or is it not?"

" 'S right, marm," stolidly answered Police-Constable Dawson.

Whereupon Aunt Hester made her entrance like Lady Macbeth.

"I am Mrs. Hester Harpenden," she announced to the walls at large. "And I have *distinctly* different information from a news-paper seller. I have—"

Here she saw Tom, who was standing in the middle of the floor.

"That's the man," she said.

Up to this time Stella (rather bucktoothed) and Dolly (distinctly pretty) had remained stupefied and silent behind the counter. Now both of them gave tongue.

"Disgusting place, eh?" cried Dolly. "I like that!"

"Busted the door, officer," screamed Stella. "Busted the door, that's what she done!"

"Busted the door, did she?" repeated Police-Constable Dawson, in a sinister voice. "Oh, ah. I see." And he reached for his note-book.

Meanwhile, as Aunt Hester calmly advanced, Tom glanced back towards Jenny.

But Jenny was not there. She was gone; she was not anywhere in the place.

The sharp pang this gave him was not his only feeling. For an instant he believed he had strayed from St. Paul's churchyard into a world of monsters and twilight, where anything might happen; and, in a sense, he was not far wrong.

"Young man," Aunt Hester asked quietly, "where is my niece?"

"Do you see her here, madam?"

"No. But that does not mean . . . A back entrance! Ah, yes! Where is the back entrance here?"

"Just a moment," said Tom, stepping in front of her. "Have you a warrant to search these premises?"

"Do I need a warrant to find my own niece?"

"Yes, yer do and all!" screamed Stella. "Either yer orders tea and cakes, which is wot we're 'ere for, or out yer go straightaway. 'S right, officer?"

" 'S right, miss," agreed the law.

Aunt Hester was not fooled for a moment.

Seen close at hand, she was—or seemed—less formidable than bitter and bony, with a high-bridge nose and washed-out blue eyes, as though she had suffered some disappointment in youth and never forgotten it. Tom could tell her clothes were fashionable, as Jenny's were fashionable, without knowing why he knew.

"Then you are all against me, it seems," she smiled. "Well! This will indeed make a budget of news for my friend the Commissioner of Police!"

"By the way," Tom said casually, "who did you say is the Commissioner of Police?"

"But Sir Richard Tringham, of course!"

"Oh, put a sock in it," said Tom. "Sir Richard Tringham has been dead for seven years. The present Commissioner is Colonel Thomas Lockwood. And I ought to know—he's my father."

"Cor!" whispered Dolly.

" 'S right, marm," agreed Police-Constable Dawson.

Aunt Hester, not in the least impressed, merely raised her shoulders.

"Ah, well!" she smiled. "If police-officers are bribed to tell untruths, then I had better be off."

Majestically she strolled towards the front of the shop. With a gesture of contempt she opened her purse, took out a couple of pound notes, and murmured something about paying for the glass door as she tossed the notes towards Stella.

Then, when she was within a step of the door, she whirled round and screamed at Tom like a harpy.

"Where is my niece?"

And Tom's temper crashed over too, like the glass platform of cakes which Dolly had been nervously handling.

"In a place where you'll never find her," he yelled back, only hoping he was telling the truth.

"If I prefer charges of abduction—"

"When she goes away of her own free will? Don't talk rot! And shall I tell you something else, Mrs. Harpenden?"

"By all means. If you can."

"That girl is of age," said Tom, advancing towards her. "Even under French law, her guardian no longer has any authority over her. But she doesn't seem to know that. She's being pushed and bullied and hounded into a marriage she doesn't want, by a lot of ghouls who are only interested in her money. And I tell you straight: I mean to stop it."

"Ah, I see. You want her money."

The steamy room was dead quiet, with fragments of shattered glass and coloured cakes all over the counter and floor. Both Stella and Dolly had cowered back.

"Yes, that hurt," said Tom. "You knew it would hurt. All right: if you want open war, it's war from this time on. Agreed?"

"Oh, agreed," replied Aunt Hester, her head high. "And I have a feeling, dear Mr. Lockwood, that you are not going to win. Good day."

With all the honors she marched out, closed the door, and turned right toward Paternoster Row. They had time to see a brown-haired girl of seventeen or eighteen, with slanting eyes and a mischievous look, run after her. It could only have been Jenny's cousin Margot.

Tom, exasperated to see those two pound notes lying on the counter, flung down another two to match them.

"That's for the smashed container and the cakes," he said.

"But, reolly, now!" protested Dolly, in an ultra-refined voice. "This is too much money. And is the Commissioner of Police reolly your father?"

" 'S right, miss," said Police-Constable Dawson, and stolidly marched out.

"Ducks, ducks, ducks!" cried Stella, addressing Tom. Being not very pretty, she was more inclined to sympathize with his bedevilments. "You needn't worry about your young lady. 'Course there's another way out of 'ere!"

"There is?"

" 'Course there is. At the back, and turn sideways. I saw your young lady run out as soon as we heard the old witch's voice outside. Either the young lady's still hiding in the passage past the washroom, or she's gorn out into Paternoster Row."

"My deepest thanks!" said Tom.

He turned and plunged towards the back—only to be stopped

short by another figure materializing in this extraordinary tea shop.

This was a shortish, wiry man with his light-brown hair cropped close to the head after a prevailing American fashion. He was perhaps in his middle thirties; he wore loose-fitting clothes, and his tie could be seen at sixty paces in any crowd.

"Now hold it, brother!" he urged. "Don't go busting out of there or you'll louse up the whole deal."

Tom blinked at him.

"The old lady," continued the stranger, evidently referring to Aunt Hester, "left her car—it would be a limousine—parked in Paternoster Row. It's not there now. She'll be screaming for the cops again, and you'll run smack into her. Besides, the kid is safe now."

"The kid? You mean Jenny? Where is she?"

Something like a self-satisfied smile crept across the newcomer's face.

"I told the chauffeur," he said, "to drive her straight to a guy named Sir Henry Merrivale, at an address he seemed to know. Sit down for a minute, until the old dame stops yelling about her stolen car."

Tom Lockwood extended his hand.

"Maybe you won't want to shake hands," retorted the newcomer almost evilly, and put his hands behind his back, "when you hear what I am."

There was about him something distinctly foreign, in a way that no American is ever foreign. Though Tom could not analyze it, his companion enlightened him.

"Get it?" he asked. "I'm a Canadian. Lamoreux's the name— Steve Lamoreux. I was born in Montreal; I can speak French as well as I speak English. In Paris they say my accent is terrible; but they understand me. I'm a newsman for L'Oeil. Been in France for six months. Don't you get it now?"

"Well! I . . ."

Steve Lamoreux's shrewd brown eyes, in the hard yet sympathetic face, were almost glaring at him. And Lamoreux spoke bitterly.

"I'm the stooge," he said. "I'm the tail. In other words, I'm Armand de Senneville's hired spy to keep out of the way, never let the girl see me, but make sure she doesn't meet any boy friends. If she does . . ."

Tom, aware that both Stella and Dolly were listening with all their ears, raised his voice.

"Could we have two more teas, please?" he called. Then, to Lamoreux: "Into the booth here. And keep your voice low."

They sat down opposite each other.

"What the hell?" said Lamoreux. "I'm only human. That girl's too innocent; I won't see her pushed around. What's more, I can't take this miracle stuff any longer—not for a hundred bucks a week or anything else. Do you realize that, but for a thousand-to-one chance, she'd be lying dead at the mortuary this very minute?"

It was a cold and ugly statement, just as the great bell of St. Paul's boomed out the hour of five.

"She didn't tell you how bad it was last night, did she?" asked Lamoreux.

"Not the details, no."

"No, you bet she didn't! The girl has guts—I'll say that for her."

"But how do you know she didn't tell me?"

"Because I overheard every word you two said in here! Look!" persisted Lamoreux, tapping a finger into his palm. "When they started out today, in their grand limousine, I followed in a taxi. Aunt Hester knows me, and knows all about me. Her husband, Uncle Fred, and young Margot—well, they've seen me once, here in England. I couldn't help that, but they'd never seen me before, and it doesn't matter. Jenny doesn't, and mustn't, even suspect.

"Those were my orders from young de Senneville. He didn't

dare send a Frenchman as a tail—it might be too conspicuous. But Jenny's seen this map of mine more than once at the newspaper office; if she spotted me, it might shake her faith in good old Armand."

"Quiet!" Tom warned softly.

It was Dolly who appeared, demurely, setting down two mugs of tea already sugared. Though she seemed inclined to linger, Lamoreux's glance sent her away miffed.

"Armand de Senneville," Tom said between his teeth. "What I should like to do to that . . . !"

"Easy, now, brother! You're talking about my boss."

"He may not be your boss much longer. You may get a better one."

"How's that? Say it again."

"Never mind; get on with the story."

"Well! Aunt Hester and Margot and Jenny had the car parked in Paternoster Row. They told the chauffeur to wait there. I ditched my taxi, and sat in the car with the chauffeur. We could see the whole front of St. Paul's. We knew we could see 'em come out."

"And then?"

"You know what happened. About thirty-five minutes later, she comes tearing down the steps. You grab her. I think to myself, 'Steve, this is your job; this is where the balloon goes up.' Over you come to this place. I sneak in the back way, and I'm practically against a matchboard partition behind you. When I heard about a voice speaking in the whispering gallery, when no voice could have spoken, I damn near fainted. And there's another thing."

"Yes?"

Uneasily Lamoreux drew out a packet of Yellow French cigarettes. He struck an old-fashioned sulphur match; he brooded while holding the match until the sulphur burned away. Then, still lost in thought, he lit the cigarette and flicked away the match.

"When I first got a gander at you, see—" Lamoreux stopped.

"Well? What is it?"

"I thought it was an ordinary pick-up. Then, when I heard you two talking, I thought you were a right guy. And I still think so."

They glared at each other, because no man pays a compliment to another's face. Then, after an embarrassed pause:

"That's why I stuck my neck out. I could see Aunt Hester charging for this joint before either of you two did. I knew Jenny would duck for a way out. And she knew the car was parked just beside here. So I rushed out and told Pearson—that's the chauffeur—to drive her straight to this guy H.M. I'd heard of the old—the old gentleman; and I knew he was all right."

Lamoreux pointed his cigarette at Tom with grimacing emphasis.

"But get this!" he added. "I'm no guardian angel or preux chevalier. The hell with that stuff. Somebody in dead earnest tried to bump off that kid. Somebody'll try again, and I want no part of it. All I'd like to know, for the sweet suffering Moses's sake, is who's doing this and why?"

Lamoreux's voice rose up piercingly until he remembered they were in public.

Then it sank to a whisper. They sat and thought and worried.

"Armand de Senneville—" Tom began.

"Look," the other said wearily. "You've got that guy on the brain. De Senneville wants to marry her for her money. What good is it to him if she's knocked off here in England?"

"Yes. I suppose that's true."

"But take it the other way round!" argued Lamoreux. "Take that gang in their country house near Hampton Court. I don't doubt Aunt Hester, at least, will get a large slice of dough when this marriage comes off. She's been in France dozens of times—she's cheering for matrimony like nobody's business. All right! Then what motive has she, or any of 'em, to kill Jenny and lose the money themselves?"

Steve Lamoreux at last took a sip of tea, which so disgusted him he did not speak for thirty seconds.

"It's nuts!" he said. "It makes no sense however you look at it."

"On the contrary," said Tom, "it's got to make sense! That's why you and I are going to see H.M. as fast as a taxi can take us."

"But I can't go there!"

"Why not?"

"Because Jenny's there, and she might spot me. All the same, if you want to reach me at any time before seven this evening, call me up at this number. If you want me any time after that, here's the number of my hotel near their house."

With a little gold pencil he scribbled two telephone numbers on a sheet torn from a notebook, and handed it to Tom.

"Locked rooms!" said Lamoreux. "Whispering voices! No motives! Brother, I'd give my last dime to go with you! What's the old—what's Sir Henry going to say about this one?"

In little more than twenty minutes, Tom Lockwood found out.

"Y'see," said Sir Henry Merrivale, with surprising meekness, "I'm sort of in trouble with the government."

"How do you mean?" asked Tom.

"Well, sort of," said H.M.

The old sinner, all sixteen stone of him, sat behind the desk in the familiar office, twiddling his thumbs over his corporation. His shell-rimmed spectacles were pulled down on his broad nose, and light from the windows behind him glistened on his bald head. On his face was the look of such martyrdom that it had won Jenny's complete sympathy and only enraged Tom.

"Well, y'see," H.M. pursued, "I've been abroad for maybe two or three years . . ."

"Ah, yes!" said Tom. "It was in New York, wasn't it, that you wrecked the subway at Grand Central Station and nabbed the right murderer on the wrong evidence?"

"Oh, son! I dunno what you're talkin' about," said H.M., giving him an austere look.

"And in Tangier, I think, you blew up a ship and let the real criminal escape just because you happened to like him?"

"Y'see how they treat me?" H.M. demanded, his powerful voice rising as he addressed Jenny. "They've got no respect for me, not a bit."

"Poor man!" Jenny said warmly.

"Oh, Lord," moaned Tom. Like most people, he could never resist the temptation to make fun of the great man; and then, to his astonishment, he found women sympathizing with H.M.'s most outrageous exploits.

"But why," he persisted, "are you in trouble with the government?"

"It seems I spent more money than I should have, or burn me, than I can account for. It also seems—would you believe it?—I shouldn't have had banking accounts in New York, Paris, Tangier, and Milan."

"You didn't know, of course, you weren't allowed to have those banking accounts?"

"Me?"

"Never mind," said Tom, smiting his forehead. "What happened to you?"

"Oh, Lord love a duck!" said H.M. "When I got back to England, you'd have thought I was Guy Fawkes and the Cato Street conspirators all rolled into one. They hoicked me up on the carpet before an old friend of mine. I won't say who this louse is, except to tell you he's the Attorney-General."

"No," said Tom. "By all means don't breathe a word."

" 'Henry,' he says to me, 'I've got you over a barrel.' "

"Did the Attorney-General actually use those words?"

"Well . . . now!" said the great man, making a broad gesture and giving Tom a withering look. "I'm tellin' you the gist of it, that's all. 'Henry,' he says, 'on the evidence I have here I could have you fined a hundred thousand pounds or stuck in jail for practically a century.'" Here H.M. broke off and appealed to Jenny. "Was this just?" he demanded.

"Of course it wasn't!" cried Jenny.

"'However,' he says, 'you pay up in full, with a fine, and we'll forget it. *Provided*,' he says—"

"Provided what?"

"I'm to go back to my own office here, d'ye see? It used to be part of the War Office, before they messed everything about in the war. And I'm to be in charge of Central Office Eight of the Metropolitan Police."

"Please," said Jenny in her soft voice, "but what is Central Office Eight?"

"It's me," H.M. replied simply. "Anybody who calls it The Ministry of Miracles is going to get a thick ear. They had enough fun, curse 'em, with the late Ministry of Information. If anything rummy turns up at Scotland Yard—any loony case that doesn't make sense—they chuck it at my head."

Here H.M.'s expression changed.

"Y'know," he said, "strictly among ourselves, I don't mind so much. I'm gettin' old and mellow now—"

"I'll bet you are," Tom muttered sardonically under his breath.

"—and it's comfortable here, sort of. Well!" said H.M., sitting up briskly and rubbing his hands together. "The old man's in business again. You got any miracles you want explained?"

"Have we!" said Tom. "Jenny! Haven't you told him?"

He himself had just arrived, hurrying in to find H.M. pouring out his woes and tribulations. In the old dusty office, high above Whitehall, Tom and Jenny looked at each other.

That office, as H.M. had said, was comfortable. Above the fireplace still hung the Satanic portrait of Fouché, Minister of Police under Napoleon. There was a very impressive-looking safe, inscribed IMPORTANT STATE DOCUMENTS: *DO NOT TOUCH!*—but containing only a bottle of whiskey. The office had seen many strange things happen—it would see many more.

"I told him about what happened in the whispering gallery, yes!" said Jenny. "But I do not even know how I have come here at all! I hated to leave you in the tea shop, but Aunt Hester was so furious I could only run. Then, at the car, the chauffeur says that some Canadian gentleman—"

"That's all right. I can explain later."

"Some Canadian gentleman, who has been sitting with him in the car when we went into St. Paul's, told him to drive me straight to this H.M. of yours. You have said so too, so I go." Jenny's brow wrinkled. "And I was so, so wrong about your H.M.!"

"Oh?" enquired Tom.

"Yes, yes! He does not swear or carry on or throw people out of windows. He is what you call a poppet."

"Hem!" said the great man modestly.

"Frankly," said Tom, eyeing the stuffed owl across the desk, "I shouldn't call it a well-chosen word to apply to him. You'll find out. However! When I'd chucked out Aunt Hester, with the aid of two counter-girls and a friendly cop, I thought I'd never get here. I was afraid some infernal thing or other had happened to you, and I might never see you again."

"You may see me," said Jenny, and stretched out her hands, "whenever you wish."

"*Oi!*" interposed a thunderous voice.

The alleged poppet was now glaring at them with a malignancy which raised Jenny's hair.

"There's not goin' to be any canoodling in this office, is there?" he demanded. "All my life I've tripped over young people with no idea except to canoodle. Now listen to me, my dolly."

His big voice altered and sharpened. The whole atmosphere of the office changed as his small eyes narrowed behind the spectacles.

He might be irascible, unreasonable, and childish, but he was still the Old Maestro—and you trifled with him at your own risk.

So H.M. spoke gently.

"You understand, my dolly, what I've already told you? That neither Général de Senneville nor Armand de Senneville has any hold over you? And neither have Aunt Hester and Company? That you're a perfectly free woman?"

Jenny pressed her hands against her cheeks.

"Yes," she said. "I suppose I always knew that, really. But . . ."

"But what?"

"People are so determined. They don't yield a bit. And it's always gone on like that. So you say to yourself, 'Oh, what's the use?' "

"Yes, I know," nodded H.M. "But that's what causes so much unhappiness in this world, especially for gals. Well, what's your feeling now? Do you want to fight 'em and beat 'em hands down?"

"Yes!"

"Do you still want to go on staying at your Aunt Hester's house? What's-its-name? Near Hampton Court?"

"It's called Broadacres, on the river. Tomorrow, they tell me, they will save the best of the sights for last—they say they will take me to see Hampton Court Palace in the afternoon."

"They say that, hey?" H.M. muttered thoughtfully. Something flickered behind his glasses and was gone. "Never mind! Do you still want to stay at your Aunt Hester's?"

"No. But what else can I do, except return to Paris?"

"Well," glowered H.M., scratching the back of his neck, "I've got a house, and a wife, and two daughters, and two good-for-nothing sons-in-law I've had to support for eighteen years. So I expect you'd better move in too."

"You mean this?" cried Jenny, and sprang to her feet. "You would really want me?" she asked incredulously.

"Bah," said H.M.

"Sir H.M.! How to thank you I do not know . . . !"

"Shut up," said the great man austerely.

Jenny sat down again.

"Then there's your clothes," he mused. "That's a very fetchin' outfit you've got on now, and I expect you brought a whole trunkful?"

"Yes, my clothes! I forget!"

"Don't worry," said H.M. with a suggestion of ghoulish mirth. "I'll send a police-officer to fetch 'em. If that doesn't put the breeze up Aunt Hester to a howlin' gale, I don't know her kind. But understand this, my dolly!"

Again his tone sharpened and struck.

"Aunt Hester'll hit back. Don't think she won't. Also, you're likely to have the whole de Senneville tribe here and on your neck." H.M. blinked at Tom. "I say, son. Shall you and I handle 'em?"

"With pleasure!" said Tom. "And definitely without gloves."

"In the meantime," H.M. went on, looking very hard at Jenny, "I've heard about this rummy business in the whispering gallery, yes. But there's something else you've got to tell me, and very clearly, before I can help you at all."

"Just a minute!" interrupted Tom.

"Oh, for the love of Esau," howled H.M. "What's wrong now?"

"A voice spoke where no voice could possibly have spoken," said Tom. "Do you believe that?"

"Certainly."

"Then how was it done?"

"Oh, my son!" groaned H.M., with a pitying glance. "You don't mean to say that trick fooled you?"

"Do you know how it was done?"

"Sure I do."

"Then what's the explanation?"

"I'm not goin' to tell you."

Tom got up and did a little dance round his chair. H.M. sternly ordered him back into it.

"I'm not goin' to tell you," he went on with dignity, "because very shortly I'm goin' to *show* you. You can see with your own eyes. That's fair enough, hey?"

Whereupon his own eyes narrowed as he looked at Jenny.

"Stop a bit! We don't want Aunt Hester to pick up the trail too soon. You said you came here in a car, with a chauffeur. Is the car still waiting? Or did you send it back?"

"I have sent it back," retorted Jenny. "But I *know* I can trust Pearson—he is the chauffeur. I have told him to say I have gone off on my own, alone, to have tea at Lyons'."

"Which Lyons'?"

Jenny's gray eyes opened wide.

"I am English, I keep telling you!" she insisted. "But how can I know much of England if I am never here? Is there more than one Lyons'? The only London restaurants of which I have heard are Lyons' and the Caprice and the Ivy."

"Those three grand old restaurants!" exclaimed Tom, and resisted an impulse to put his arms 'round her. "H.M., Aunt Hester will think Jenny is giving her the raspberry, which is exactly what you'd do yourself."

"Uh-huh. That'll do. Now then: about this first miracle—of a gas-tap being turned on in a locked room."

When H.M. produced his ancient black pipe, and began to load it with tobacco looking (and tasting) like the steel wool used on kitchen sinks, Tom knew he must brace himself for more trouble.

"My dolly," said H.M., "a lot of bits and pieces have come flyin' out of your story. I can see this aunt of yours. I can see her daughter, Margot, who's eighteen years old and up to mischief. I can see your Uncle Fred, who's tall and red-faced and looks like a retired major. I can see this white Georgian house, with long windows, set back from the river. But burn me if I can see the details!"

"How do you mean?"

"For instance. D'ye usually sleep with the windows closed, to say nothin' of being locked? Is that an old French custom?"

"No, no, of course not!"

"Well, then?"

"It is the details," said Jenny, biting her lip, "I have not wished to talk about. They are—bad. I feel the gas strangle me again. But never mind! First, Aunt Hester put me into a bedroom on the ground floor."

"Why?"

"And why not?" Jenny exclaimed reasonably. "It is a very nice room. But it has two windows stretching to the ground. Aunt Hester is frightened of burglars, and asks me please to keep the windows tight-locked. By the time I am ready for bed, I am so scared that I put both bolts on the door as well—on the inside. You see, it was at dinner I received the note."

"What note?"

"It was a little note, folded up in my napkin at the table. I thought—"

"Yes, my dolly?"

"At first," Jenny explained, peeping sideways at Tom, "I thought it was from a young man I met at a tea party they gave. He has made what you call the eyes at me. So—"

"*That's* an old French custom, if you like," Tom said politely. "You thought the note was from him, and you didn't want anybody else to know?"

Jenny turned on him flaming.

"I do not like this young man at the tea party! I do not wish to see him again! But if he has written a note to me, can I give the poor man away?"

"No. Sorry, Jenny. Shouldn't have said that."

"But it is not from him at all, or anything like that. I read it under the table. It was only one line, in a handwriting I never saw before. It said, '*You will die tonight, Jennifer.*' "

Jenny moistened her lips. H.M. had lighted the pipe, and an oily cloud of smoke crept over the desk.

"At first I thought it was a joke. What else can I think? Then I looked at the rest of them, all so normal, with the candles burning on the dinner table. And I know I am alone. I am a stranger, even if I am in my own country—and I am frightened!

"I did not even dare ask if the note was a joke. So I hid it, and afterwards I lost it. At eleven o'clock, when it was time to go to bed . . ."

"Yes, my dolly? Go on!"

"I sleep badly," said Jenny. "Always I have. No matter how late I go to bed, I always wake up at 5 or 5:30 in the morning. There was a custom I had in France, first when I lived with my parents and afterwards at the house of Général de Senneville. A maid brought me a cup of chocolate at six in the morning.

"When Aunt Hester asked if she could do anything more, I asked if I might have the chocolate, or else tea, at that time. I had been there several days, but it was the first time I venture to ask. Aunt Hester lifts her eyebrows and says, 'Do you think, Jennifer my dear, that is quite fair to the servants?'

"I said no, no, please to forget it. But Margot, who has green eyes and is nice, she is always up before six, she says, and will be glad to bring me a cup of tea then. Very well! I go to my room. I turn on the light. I fasten the bolts both at the top and bottom of the door. Then I turn round. And one of the windows, which I have left locked, is wide open."

Jenny paused.

H.M., wrapped in his cloud of nauseous smoke, was as expressionless as an idol.

"I rush across," continued Jenny, her voice rising. "I close and lock the window again. Then I think, 'Suppose someone is hiding in the room?' But I must not be stupid and rouse the whole house. And so—well! I search the room myself. Nobody is hiding there. I think perhaps some servant has opened the window to air the room, and I feel better.

"It is a warm night—very warm, they tell me, for an English spring. So I do not need to turn on the gas heater in the fireplace when I undress. I close the window curtains almost shut. But I smoke a cigarette or two, you can bet, before I have the nerve to turn out the light. But I do turn out the light, finally. And soon I am asleep. Then—"

"Hold on!" interposed H.M. softly, and took the pipe out of his mouth.

"Y-yes?"

"What time did you turn in? Do you remember?"

"Yes. I see my wrist watch. It is ten minutes past twelve."

"Did any of this family know beforehand about your habit of takin' chocolate at six in the morning?"

"N-no, I do not think so. How could they? I—"

Again Jenny was trembling; and, worst sign of all, she was again glancing over her shoulder. Tom got up and put his hands on her shoulders.

"Hadn't we better stop this, H.M.?" he demanded.

"We can't stop it, son, and you know we can't. That gal really was in a locked room. It's practically impossible to tamper with bolts when they're at the top and bottom of the door. Those Georgian window-locks are dead sure for safety. Unless I can get a hint about this, the old man's dished."

"I am very well, thank you," said Jenny. "I can go on, if you wish."

"Well?" said H.M., putting the pipe back in his mouth.

"First there was a dream. It was horrible, but I don't remember it now. Then I knew I was awake, and being strangled so I could not breathe. This part is hard to describe. But—when you are dying, or even losing consciousness, you can still hear sounds clearly even though you can barely see?"

"Yes, my dolly. That's right."

"I could tell it was just growing daylight, no more. But somebody was pounding on the outside of the door. And I hear Margot's voice crying my name. I tried to scream back, but there is no breath, and already—this is not pretty—I had been sick.

"Next, which is all confused, I heard a man's voice outside with Margot. It was an American voice I have never heard before. It said, 'What's wrong, kid? Isn't she okay?' Margot screams that the room is full of gas, and can't he smell it from under the door? He says, 'You won't break down that door. Where's the window?'

"Still I am just conscious. I can hear everything, though it must be like being hanged. I hear them run away, and someone else join them. Then I see—all blurry, because my eyes have nearly gone— I see someone's fist, wrapped in a coat, punch through the glass of the far window.

"This is my Uncle Fred, who has been roused too. He unlocks the window and pushes it all the way up. Someone runs to turn off the gas-tap at the heater. I think this is the American. I cannot see, but I hear him say a wicked word, and say, 'So-and-so, but it's turned full on!' He turns it off. Margot rushes towards me, spilling a tea tray on the carpet. That is all I remember, until the doctor is there."

Jenny lifted her hands, and let them fall on the handbag in her lap. As the oily smoke from H.M.'s pipe reached her at last, she began to cough.

H.M. put down the pipe and knocked it out.

"The doctor, hey?" he repeated. "And what did the doctor say?"

"It was not the doctor who spoke to me. It was Aunt Hester. She said, 'This is not very considerate of you, Jennifer. To try to

kill yourself because you are not happy about your future husband.' "

Tom Lockwood's grip tightened on her shoulders. "Your Aunt
Hester said that?"

"Yes! And it is not true! But they ask how anyone could have
tried to kill me, when the room is all locked up inside?"

"Anything else, Jenny?"

"I say, 'Where is the American?' They say, 'What American?'
and claim he is a delusion of mine. They stand round my bed, all
big-eyed—Aunt Hester and Cousin Margot and even poor old
Uncle Fred—and look down at me. They say it is a mercy the doctor is their family doctor, and will not report this to the police.
Dear God, do you wonder I am afraid of them?"

"H.M.!" Tom said sharply, after a pause.

"Well?"

"You may have been wondering about this mysterious American . . ."

"Frankly, son, I have. I don't see where he fits in."

"He isn't an American," said Tom, "but he isn't a delusion
either. That gang made a bad slip when they claimed he was. I'll
tell you all about him at the proper time. Meanwhile, do you see
any clue at all?"

H.M., who had been sitting with his eyes closed and a very
mulish look on his face, now opened his eyes slowly and inspected
Jenny.

"My dolly," he said, "I've got only one more question to ask
now. But I want you to be awful careful how you answer it. You
could hear all these voices clearly when you were nearly unconscious. You could hear the pounding on the door, the footsteps
running away, and the rest of it. *Did you hear any other sound
besides that?*"

"What—what kind of sound?"

"Any kind!"

"No, I don't think so."

"You're sure of that, now?"

"Yes, positive!"

"Oh, Lord love a duck," observed Sir Henry Merrivale, with his mouth falling open. "So *that's* how the locked room was worked!"

"How?" shouted Tom.

"I'm the old man," said H.M., tapping himself impressively on the chest. "You let me deal with this in my own way. I'm goin' into action at once."

H.M. reached for the telephone at his elbow. He dialed for an outside exchange, and then dialed the number. During a long pause, while they could hear the ringing tone go on interminably, Tom Lockwood listened to an air-vent which hummed and hummed in the ceiling, and at intervals he studied H.M.'s face, now as malignant as the Evil One's.

The ringing tone broke off. There ensued, from H.M.'s side, the following weird and wonderful conversation.

"Looky here, my wench. I want to speak to Sam. . . . Oh, yes, I can! This is the old man. You just tell him I squared it when he was givin' a beautiful party for sixteen beautiful gals without any clothes on, and the silly-ass coppers broke in. Yes, the old man! . . ."

A grateful note crept into H.M.'s big voice.

"That you, Sam? How are you . . . ? Never better, Sam! There's a question I want to ask you. . . . Thank'ee, Sam. How many vents are working now? . . ."

Tom Lockwood looked up wildly at the air-ventilator humming and whacking above his head. He looked at an equally bewildered Jenny.

"Only three? You're sure of that? Right, Sam. Gimme their names and descriptions. Yes, I said descriptions! Uh-huh. . . . No, the first one's no good. Try the second. . . . Lord love a duck,

that sounds like the one we want! But try the third, just for luck.
. . . No, he's no good either. It's Charley Johnson. Gimme the
address. It's nearly six o'clock—he's bound to be at home now. . . .
Thanks a million, Sam. And try to keep to one woman next time,
hey? All right, all right!"

Ringing off with the handsome air of one who has made all
things clear, Sir Henry Merrivale spun the dial once again.

"Sergeant? I want a squad car, to hold three people and a driver,
as quick as kiss-your-hand. Two minutes? Outside the Horse Guards
Avenue entrance? Right!"

Lumbering to his feet, H.M. took down from a rack an ancient
Panama hat and thrust it on. This hat, which had a band of startling colors and whose brim was turned down all round like a
bowl, gave an even more sinister look to the great man's unmen-
tionable face.

"Sir!" protested Tom. "What in the name of sense is all this
business of air-vents, and how can it help us?"

"You wanted a miracle explained, didn't you?" demanded the
great man. "All right. Are you comin' with me, or not?"

Within the promised two minutes, and in the police car—Jenny
and Tom sitting in the back seat, H.M. piled in front with the
chauffeur—they whipped out of Horse Guards Avenue, turned left,
and shot down Whitehall. H.M., who himself has never driven a
car without landing through a shop window or against a lamp-
post, made caustic comments about driving skill to a red-eared
police driver.

Far beyond the towers of Westminster, behind its stately terraces
and flats, lies a region of dingy, almost unknown, streets. The red-
brick houses in these streets, by a show of brass knobs and letter-
slots, try to keep up a brave pretense that they are private homes
and not lodging houses.

But gritty winds make discarded newspapers dance along their
gutters; children scream; there is an over-riding clatter of dustbins.

Before one such dingy house, which did look like a private home and really was, the car stopped.

"Come on, you two," grunted H.M.

He impelled Jenny and Tom out of the car and up a flight of stone steps to the front door. There he jabbed his finger at the bell.

"For the last time," said the desperate Tom, "will you tell what an air-vent—" H.M. pulled down the brim of his hat even harder.

"Who said anything about an air-vent?" he howled. "*I* didn't. I said 'vent.' That's the theatrical and professional term for a ventriloquist. Didn't you ever hear a ventriloquist?"

Jenny's hands flew to her open mouth.

"According to your story," pursued H.M., "there were only four persons in the whispering gallery with you. This time we can acquit both your Aunt Hester and your Cousin Margot—they were leaning over the railing, much too far away from the wall.

"We can acquit the outraged verger in charge of the place. But who else was there? According to you, a fat and red-faced countryman—a little too thoroughly dressed up as a countryman, wasn't he?—who carried a packet of sandwiches and a thermos flask.

"When you heard the words, he was sitting against the walls and plainly drinking tea. All right, my fatheads! Who's the only man alive who can make his dummy speak clearly while he himself is walloping down a full glass of water? You know the answer.

"I rang up the king of all impresarios and found out the names and descriptions of the only three vents working in London. This Charley Johnson won't know much about the case. Somebody handed him a fiver to play what he thought, and probably still thinks, was a joke. But *he*, when we see him, can tell us who bribed him to—"

The front door was hurled open.

There is no other word for it—the door crashed against the wall and all but rebounded.

In the doorway there stood, swaying slightly, that same fat man

Jenny recognized from the whispering gallery. His face was now less professionally red; he was bald, and wore no wig. Instead of his countryman's clothes, he was wrapped round in a somewhat grubby dressing gown of black and orange stripes. In one hand he held a whiskey-and-soda, in the other a half-eaten sandwich.

But what held them was the expression of his face. His eyes were so horribly wide open that a ring of white showed all the way round the iris.

"*Look out, you two!*" snapped H.M.

Tom dragged Jenny back just in time.

Charles Johnson, making a bubbling noise, took one step forward. Then he pitched headlong down the stone steps, turning over twice before he lay face down on the pavement.

The smashed glass, the half-eaten sandwich, had flown wide and fallen. Because of the man's tiger-striped dressing gown, it was a moment or two before any of them saw the black handle of the knife driven into his back just under the left shoulder blade.

Nobody moved until the police driver sprang out of the car. It did not need the driver's nod, looking up, to tell them Johnson was dead.

Children's roller skates crashed past on the opposite side of the street, amid shouting. A few windows banged up; a few women's heads were thrust out. That was all.

H.M.'s face was white.

"Easy, my dolly," he said, putting his hand on Jenny's arm and speaking with surprising gentleness. "Is that the man you saw at the whispering gallery?"

The shock was too great. Jenny could only nod.

"Then that means," said H.M., "this is no straight business of frightening a gal out of her wits. It means there's somebody who's dead-determined, crazy-mad, to get what he or she wants. Somebody got here before us and shut Johnson's mouth. Murder with a knife is all in the day's work. And that means . . ."

He brooded so long, ruffling his fingers at his temples, that Tom could not remain quiet.

"H.M.!" he said. "What is it?"

"It means there's been a slight change of plans," he answered.

"How?"

"You, my dolly," said H.M., "aren't going to spend the night at my house after all. If you've got the nerve, you're goin' straight back to spend the night at Aunt Hester's."

A golden sky was becoming tinged with purple over the thin Tudor chimneys of Hampton Court Palace.

Sir Henry Merrivale, in his most maddening mood, sat on an upended wheelbarrow, in one of the few remaining Tudor quadrangles: of dark red brick, with its white stone lions uprearing from the walls beside sly little windows. H.M. was again smoking his black pipe, and looked up at Tom without favour.

"Well," he asked querulously, "where's the whole party now?"

"As far as I know, they're still tramping through miles and miles of picture galleries."

"But looky here, son!" protested the great man. "According to my watch, and the notices posted up, this place should have been closed for a long time. Shouldn't they all have been flung out of here hours ago?"

"Yes. But it seems Uncle Fred has a lot of influence with the director or the curator or whatever they call him. They're being taken over the whole show at their leisure, particularly since Jenny's keen to see the maze; and that's a long way from here."

"Maze, hey?" H.M. repeated thoughtfully.

"Now listen to me!" roared Tom, assuming an oratorical posture. "Since a few minutes past six yesterday afternoon, when you got rid of us all, until half an hour ago, when I set eyes on your ugly dial again, you've asked questions by the bucket. But you won't answer a single question yourself. Why?"

" 'Cause I'm the old man."

"And you think that's a good enough reason?"

"Sure it is. I say, son. How is . . . I mean, how is . . . ?"

Tom regarded him bitterly.

"How is Jenny taking this?" he asked. "What the devil do you expect, after that asinine order she was to go back to Aunt Hester's last night? She's taking it badly, of course! But she won't let any of 'em see for a minute she's afraid."

Here the old sinner had at least the grace to look discomfited.

"Well . . . now!" he growled. "I had my reasons, hadn't I? Burn me," and H.M.'s voice rose up passionately, "people are always sayin', 'What an old cloth-head he is; stick him upside down in the dustbin.' Then they see what I mean. And they yell, 'Why, Henry; pull him out and dust him off; we should never have guessed it.' And of course they wouldn't have guessed it, the stargazin' goops! Only—"

H.M.'s eloquence was interrupted only by a back-wash taste from his own black pipe. Then he simply sat and looked evil.

"All right, all right!" he said. "What did you do last night?"

"Steve Lamoreux and I stood guard outside Jenny's windows all night—"

"Stop a bit, son. Does the gal know who Lamoreux is?"

"She doesn't know he's Armand de Senneville's spy, naturally! And she can't meet him. But, for all practical purposes, he isn't a spy. He won't stand for violence—"

"Uh-huh. I know. I talked to him in my office today. You were sayin'?"

"Well, while the rest of 'em were at dinner, Steve and I sneaked into her bedroom and dismantled the gas heater . . ."

Tom paused in even more exasperation. H.M., with a silent and ghoulish mirth, was rocking in ecstasy.

"Oh, son! You didn't think the murderer would try that simple little trick again?"

"*Simple* little trick?"

"Easy as shellin' peas."

"Will you acknowledge to me," demanded Tom, after a hard-breathing pause, "that the door of the room really was tightly bolted on the inside and couldn't have been tampered with?"

"Sure."

"Will you acknowledge that both windows were securely locked on the inside and that they weren't tampered with in any way?"

"Agreed without a struggle."

"Will you finally acknowledge that, with no funny business about outside gas meters or the like, somebody—somebody *actually in that room*—turned on the gas-tap?"

"That's right, son."

"*Then how in hell did the murderer get in and out of that room?*"

"I'm not goin' to tell you. Now wait!" said H.M., and pointed with the stem of his pipe. "Yesterday you raved and danced about the 'miracle' of the ventriloquist, didn't you? But that was easy. And this is just as easy, maybe easier, if you think about it. I want you to think about it. Meanwhile, you'd better think of something and somebody you've rather neglected."

"Oh? Who's that?"

"Armand de Senneville himself. You hated him from instinct and from jealousy. But maybe your instincts were right. *I* had him investigated today."

"Well?"

"He's tough, son," H.M. said somberly. "He's tougher than you think. He's an outstanding businessman, a first-class journalist, a mechanical expert, and he was liaison officer with the Yanks for four years during the war. Finally, he's as conceited as the devil; he swears, in private, there's *nothing* he ever wanted that he hasn't got."

"But Armand de Senneville's in Paris!"

"He doesn't have to be here, don't you see?" H.M. asked patiently. "Now listen. You, and the gal Jenny, and even Steve Lamoreux, have all thought there was a whole conspiracy of the Harpenden family—Uncle Fred, young Margot, and Aunt Hester —against Jenny Holden."

"And isn't there?"

"No! Coincidence has mixed you up. There's only one, one of those three, who has any knowledge of it. One of them, bribed by Armand de Senneville, would pay any price to have Jenny Holden frightened out of her wits. I give you three: which one?"

It was growing darker in the ancient quadrangle. Tom paced up and down the paving stones, his footfalls stirring back ghostly echoes from the walls.

H.M. knocked out his pipe and replaced it.

"Burn me," he said in a worried voice, "where's that whole family now? You were supposed to be keepin' track of 'em, weren't you?"

"I couldn't! Aunt Hester knows me too well, from that bang-up row in the tea shop! But Steve is trailing 'em, and giving me signals from windows whenever he can."

"But they can't stay in there forever! It'll be pitch dark! I'd give my ears to know where they've gone!"

It was unnecessary to sacrifice H.M.'s ears.

From under the archway to a second quadrangle the sound of "S-s-t!" hissed at them in a way which made H.M. leap up from the overturned wheelbarrow.

Steve Lamoreux approached as warily as a red Indian. Tom, not without difficulty, had persuaded him to put on a dark suit and an inconspicuous necktie. But his short brown hair stood up as wirily as ever, and he infuriated H.M. by addressing the great man as Pop.

"They're outside," he said, "at the back of the joint. They're going along that broad path, at the back of the palace, that runs a long way to the left between the palace and the gardens. They've got the oldest guide here, who's deaf and practically blind. And for the love of Pete, Pop, get a wiggle on or they'll close the inner gates and *we'll* be locked in!"

H.M., not without much ruffling of his dignity, was hauled and impelled through the archway, across another quadrangle, and then through a very long archway at whose end they could see the last gleam of daylight.

They stopped at the outer edge of the arch. Just ahead lay the immense gardens, their straight-ruled lines of flower beds draining of colour in twilight. Peering round the edge of the arch to the left, Tom saw the very broad, sanded path beside ancient walls.

Five persons, their backs to the conspirators in the archway, strolled along this path about a hundred yards ahead. Though it was too dark to discern faces at that distance, Tom knew who they were as they walked abreast.

First, on the extreme left, doddered an old guide in uniform. Next, marching briskly, strode Aunt Hester. Jenny walked nervously between the giggling Margot, who danced with short steps, and the firm military stride of Uncle Fred on the extreme right.

"All right," whispered Tom. "What do we do now?"

"I know what we *could* do," said Lamoreux.

"You do, hey?" sneered H.M.

"Yes! They can't recognize us in this light. If we just strolled after 'em, three abreast but keeping back, they'd take us for another privileged tourist party like themselves. That is, if somebody could do a little spiel like a guide."

The role of guide caught Sir Henry Merrivale's fancy at once.

"Hem!" he said, tapping himself on the chest. "Me."

Lamoreux looked doubtful.

"Okay, Pop, you're the boss. But are you sure you know enough about the history of this joint?"

"*Me?*" said the outraged H.M. "The palace of Hampton Court," he bellowed, "begun by Cardinal Wolsey in the year 1515, was in 1526 pinched from this worthy prelate by that howlin' old ram King Henry the Eighth, whose wives I shall now proceed to—"

"Pop! Quiet!"

"Am I a guide," H.M. asked loftily, "or ain't I?"

"You are," snapped Tom. "And if the balloon goes up, it goes up. Anyway, I can see Jenny. They can't hurt her now. Let's go."

Out they marched, trying to tread softly, with Lamoreux on the inner side, Tom in the middle, and H.M. on the outer side.

It was quiet, so intense that they could hear the footsteps of those far ahead of them as well as their own. Peace lay in the hollow of a warm spring night, with the fragrance of grass and trees. You would never have guessed that death was walking with them along the broad white path—and moving closer at every pace.

Tom Lockwood did not know this, of course. But he sensed danger-fangs everywhere. He kept his eyes fixed on Jenny as though she might disappear, and his nerves were twitching like a landed fish.

So he quite literally jumped as a mighty voice smote through his thoughts.

"On our right," it thundered, "we got the famous Hampton Court gardens, forty-four acres of elegant spinach, first laid out by King William the Third and completed in 1734."

"For God's sake be careful," whispered Tom. "William the Third died in 1702."

H.M. swung round, fists on hips.

"And d'ye think I don't know that?" he bellowed. "I didn't say the old sour-puss finished 'em, did I? I just said he laid 'em out— which is what I'm goin' to do to you, young man, if you don't shut up and stop interruptin' my lecture."

"Pop! The soft pedal! Give it the old soft pedal! Holy cats, they'll hear you as far as Thames Ditton!"

But, whatever devilment H.M. had meditated—and Tom knew

he had planned it in advance—the damage was done. Five persons, mere shapes in the twilight, turned round and looked back.

Out from the group, head high, marched Aunt Hester. She strode along the full distance that separated them, and looked straight at H.M.

"You, I fancy," she said coolly, "must be the man Merrivale?"

"On our left," bellowed H.M., "we see the celebrated tennis court. The game of tennis, originally played with a wooden ball, was designed with the laudable purpose of knockin' somebody's eye out—which it generally did. One famous match—"

"Answer me, please!" said Aunt Hester. "On whose authority, may I ask, are you in these grounds after official visiting hours?"

H.M. gave her a wicked look.

"On Sir Hugh Rossiter's," he said. "The same as yours. Want to ring him and find out?"

Since H.M. knew everybody, this might possibly be true. Aunt Hester did not dare risk the challenge. Besides, she was more interested in someone else.

"One of you, I believe," she stated crisply, "I have already met. Indeed, Mr. Lockwood, I wish to have a word with you."

"Fire away," said Tom.

"Ever since you abducted my niece yesterday, and afterwards returned her in—I *hope*—a condition suitable to a bride, poor Jennifer has been talking nonsense which I propose to stamp out here and now."

"Oh?"

"Yes. Absurdly enough, the girl believes she is in love with you . . ."

"Is she, by God!" exclaimed Tom.

Whereupon he completely lost his head. Raising his voice, he shouted clearly and loudly through the twilight.

"*Jenny!*" he called. "*Jenny! Do you love me?*"

Jenny spun round in the broad white path.

"Yes!" she shouted back.

"*Will you marry me?*"

"Yes!"

Dead silence.

"Well . . . now!" observed Sir Henry Merrivale, with much complacence. "Since that's all settled and finished—"

"Oh, cripes!" breathed Steve Lamoreux, in a voice Tom had never heard him use. "If that's how people propose to each other in England, maybe it's true you're kind of casual. Do you just get married on the telephone, or what?"

But Aunt Hester was not amused. The paint stood out against her pale face; she was alert, smiling—and dangerous.

"How interesting!" She laughed. "It surely will interest her dear guardian and," Aunt Hester's eyes slid sideways, "the fiancé to whom she is pledged. Tell me, Mr. Lockwood, what is your yearly income?"

Tom stared at the ground.

"Well! I didn't want to . . ."

"Come, Mr. Lockwood!" said Aunt Hester, with honeyed sweetness. "You are a reporter on the *Record*, we know. Just what *is* your yearly income?"

"Tell her, son," growled H.M.

"All right!" said Tom, raising his head. "When death duties are subtracted, it'll be about twelve thousand pounds a year."

"Twelve—thou—"

"I didn't earn it," snapped Tom. "My mother left it to me. I've published just one unsuccessful novel. When I walked up Ludgate Hill yesterday, I was thinking about chucking my job and trying full-time writing. That's what I'll do, when Jenny marries me. It's why I told you, Steve, you might get a better boss; you can have my job, and they'll hand it to you on a plate. But I've never given two hoots about Jenny's money, and I'd rather prefer it if she didn't have a penny to her name."

"This is the most fantastic—" Aunt Hester was beginning, when she stopped dead.

H.M. slowly extended his neck, and gave her such a look as could not have been matched by Satan himself.

"Madam," he said, "you've got no business with us. Sling your hook."

"I absolutely refuse—"

H.M. extended his finger until it almost touched Aunt Hester's nose.

"Madam," he said, "are you goin' to hop it? Or do you prefer to find yourself, sittin' down, in the middle of King William's spinach?"

Aunt Hester hopped it. Before that glare, which would have caused the Angels of Light themselves to retire to prepared positions, she could have done nothing else.

She ran hard towards the group ahead, and appeared to be talking rapidly. The whole group faced round and began hurrying, at a faster pace, in their original direction. Jenny seemed violently to object, but Margot gripped her arm and hastened her on.

Tom Lockwood, a powerfully built young man, was all for charging forward and starting a fight at once. His companions held him back.

"Easy, son!" said H.M. "Not just yet, I tell you! We've got 'em in sight. They can't get away."

"Pop," declared Lamoreux, whose face was pale and pinched, "you're a so-and-so. You're a so-and-so and a this-and-that. You deliberately yelled all that guff about spinach and tennis balls, just so the old dame would come tearing back here. Why did you do it?"

"Well . . . now!" said H.M. with a modest look. "I rather wanted to know, d'ye see, if some person would meet some other person. Am I making myself clear?"

"No. You're not."

"Never mind, son," soothed H.M. "I haven't been so much worried about that gal as about another person. Besides, I repeat, they can't get away. We've got 'em in sight."

Lamoreux stopped in his tracks.

"Oh, no, we haven't!" he said in a high voice. "Where are they now? They've disappeared!"

It was true.

Once past the gardens and the long line of the palace, the road was closed in by tall trees, dusky and spectral against a windless night, with an occasional bench on either side. Five persons had vanished from the road.

"H.M.," said Tom, seizing his companion's arm, "you seem to be the expert on Hampton Court. Where does this road lead?"

"Steady, son! It leads to one of the main entrances—the Lion Gate. But, if you turn to the left before you reach the gate, you'll soon get to the open space where they've got the maze—"

"The maze!" said Tom, and every nameless fear boiled up inside him. "Run, you blighters! *Run!*"

That H.M. himself did run, despite his large corporation and his dislike of any pedestrian exercise, can only be stated as a fact. Lifting his chin so as to cleave the air, he belted along that road as fast as his younger companions.

Some hundred and twenty yards farther on, they saw the dim gleam of a light past an avenue of trees branching to the left. Into this they flew abreast, found themselves in a large open space, and stopped.

For the first time they heard the wheezing, rusty voice of the old guide.

"Now, miss," he was pleading, "you don't really want to go into the maze, do you? 'Tisn't very difficult, not what we like to pretend it is. But that's in the daytime. You don't want to go in at night, miss."

"But I do!" Jenny insisted firmly. "All my life I've been reading about the Hampton Court maze, and I'll die if I don't explore it. Won't you lend me your electric torch?"

In the clearing, a hut or small pavilion had been set well back, evidently used as somebody's living quarters; on a pole against the side of the hut burned a sickly electric bulb.

The famous maze was set well out from the hut. It was roughly oval in shape, a little higher than a man's head, of green hedge raggedly trimmed. Illumined in bright green and dead shadow by the sickly light, it loomed up less as a place of comedy than as a secret, malicious trap.

The entrance must be at the far side, because the entire party was assembled there. Slant-eyed Margot was jumping up and down with joy.

"May I go in too, Mama?" she shrilled. "May I go?"

"No, you may not," said Aunt Hester sharply. "Afterwards, perhaps, if dear Jennifer—"

"Lot of nonsense, I call it," grumbled Uncle Fred from under his gray military moustache.

"Please may I have the electric torch?" said Jenny in a voice no man could resist.

"Ah, well," mumbled the guide. " 'Ere's the torch. I s'pose I can always climb up on top of the stepladder by the entrance, and give you directions if you get lost. Be nippy, now."

"I will! I will!"

"Jenny!" called Tom. "Jenny, wait! I'm going with you!"

His words did not carry to her. Faintly he heard the creak of a small gate, and the brushing of Jenny's body against the narrow sides of the maze.

Tom sprang forward. Instantly Sir Henry Merrivale locked both his arms from behind, and held him back.

"No, son," said H.M., in so soft and deadly a voice that Tom was startled. "You're not goin' into that maze."

"Why not?"

"Whose life," asked H.M., glancing round him, "d'ye think I've been worried about, as much or more than the little gal's herself? Yours."

"Are you crazy?"

"No. But you're not goin' inside that maze."

Tom, with one sudden heave and jerk, tore loose even from H.M.'s powerful grip.

"I'm sorry, sir. But that's where I'm going, and neither you nor anybody else is going to stop me."

He ran across the sanded space, and round the side to the entrance. He saw the startled face of Uncle Fred, who was swinging a heavy yellow cane. He saw Aunt Hester, with rigid mouth. He saw the pretty, mischievous face of Margot, who was slipping away in another direction.

The guide had already shakily mounted to the top of the stepladder beside the entrance. Tom swung open the little gate, twisted sideways as he plunged into the maze, and attempted to run.

It was impossible.

The hedge-walls were so narrow that tendrils stung his face. Though it was not pitch-dark, just enough light filtered down from the dim bulb outside to distort the eyesight and turn dark shapes into illusions. He might run slap into a hedge-wall at any second, and just saved himself from doing so.

Gently, now!

Stopping at a turn, Tom felt down on his left and found the thin wall, of hard and curved wire, built a little below waist height. In this maze, he remembered it had been said, you must always turn to the left. He did so, and presently turned left again.

That was when he saw, deeper inside these thinnish walls, the firefly glimmer of Jenny's torch. It vanished again—but it was there.

"Jenny!" he called. "Wait for me! It's Tom!"

"Tom! Darling!" Her voice slipped through the walls rather than above them. "Where are you?"

"I don't know. Where are you?"

"Very near the center of the maze, I think."

"Then stop where you are! Wait until I catch up with you!"

"Oh, no!" Jenny retorted demurely. "I'll get to the center and turn off the torch. Then you can find me and tell me how much you love me."

"Jenny, wait!"

But the firefly glimmer danced away. He could hear her brushing and hurrying on. In a moment or two there was a cry of pleasure, as evidently she found the center of the maze. The light of her torch went out.

Tom moved forward, more slowly and carefully. The electric bulb at the hut was now so distant and so dim that it gave scarcely any light. Tom didn't know where he was. Walls loomed up and closed round him. It wasn't pleasant, being shut into a twisting maze where . . .

Then he stopped, listening.

Somebody was following him stealthily through the maze.

Somebody, not much lighter than his own weight, was stalking him—with what intent? Tom ran forward and stopped. The footsteps behind him ran forward and stopped. Tom ran again. But he was not left in doubt long.

A closer footfall, a looming of a shape in near-darkness, made him glance over his shoulder. He saw the upsurge of someone's silhouette. A distant gleam flashed on the blade of the knife as if lifted high—and struck.

All that saved Tom from being stabbed in the back, as Johnson the ventriloquist had been stabbed, was the dim light and the attacker's misjudgment. The blade of the knife ripped through the

cloth of the coat over Tom's shoulder. The attacker, plunging forward so hard that he collided with Tom, sent his victim sprawling
one way and drove his own head and shoulders, grotesquely,
straight into the hedge on the other side.

Somebody screamed one word, nothing more.

With a crackling of branches, the attacker wrenched out his left
arm and then withdrew his head. Before he could disengage his
knife-hand, Tom landed a vicious right-hander that opened his as-
sailant's cheekbone and drew first blood.

Then they faced each other, two dim shapes, between the narrow walls.

There were no Queensberry Rules here. Neither man was a
boxer. But both were enraged and both meant murder.

The attacker held his knife blade out, to leap forward and rip up.
Just as he lunged, Tom kicked him in the groin. The attacker, in
intense agony, began to double up; his knife fell and tinkled. Tom
hit him again.

The attacker, straightening up, flew in with both fists. Tom hit
him twice, left and right, in the belly. Then he put all his strength
into a right cross to the man's jaw—which, if it had landed, would
have broken Tom's hand.

But it did not land on the jaw. Instead it landed, with just as
murderous effect, in the soft flesh under the man's left ear. The
attacker, brain paralyzed and legs suddenly gone to water, reeled
backwards and fell.

"Now where the devil," Tom was thinking, "did we get so much
space?"

Then he realized they had been fighting very near the entrance
to the center of the maze. For the first time he heard voices, and
bodies thrashing about in the maze.

Behind him loomed up the blaze of an electric torch. Above it
showed the malignant countenance of Sir Henry Merrivale. Next,

cowering away in one side of the maze's center, Jenny switched on her own torch.

Both beams converged on the man who lay on his back in the center of the maze. His eyes were closed; he breathed stertorously; sluggish blood flowed from a cut in his cheek.

Jenny's face grew so white, and she turned her head away so abruptly, that Tom thought she was going to be sick.

But his own feelings were swallowed up in incredulity.

"This is impossible!" he said, pointing to the man on the ground. "That's Steve Lamoreux, the reporter!"

"*Oh, no, it's not,*" said Sir Henry Merrivale. "*That's Armand de Senneville himself.*"

"Explanations?" demanded H.M., in a tone of dismal surprise. "You don't mean to tell me you *need* explanations?"

Jenny and Tom, both seated beside the desk in H.M.'s office at the end of the following day, instantly and vehemently said they did need explanations.

H.M. sighed.

"Y'know, my dolly," he said, "you ought to have seen through your fiancé, Armand de Senneville, sooner than you did. He tried to prevent your trip to England. He couldn't prevent it—his father's word was law. But he knew how much you'd been repressed and kept under the thumb in France. He knew, as he casually warned Aunt Hester, you'd probably fall bang for the first presentable, easy-going Englishman who made you laugh and didn't think correct behavior was everything in life. Which is what you did."

"I did not!" Jenny cried indignantly. "I have fall bang for Tom, yes. But that is a different thing!"

Tom hastily intervened in order to evade the devastating question, "How is it different?"

"Then de Senneville," he said, "had only to crop his hair, have it dyed brown, wear very loud clothes, and pose as a French-Canadian reporter from one of his own papers?"

"But Armand," insisted Jenny, "speaks no English!"

"No?" said H.M. "That's what he told you, my dolly. But as I explained to Tom here, the bloke was attached for four years to the American Army as a liaison officer. So surely he could speak English. In fact, his ear was perfect; his American was perfect. But he had to play the part of a French Canadian to explain how he spoke both languages."

"And yet," exclaimed Jenny, her eyes clouding, "I still do not understand this Armand! If he wished to keep men away from me, why did he not say he spoke English and go with the whole party of us?"

"You don't understand that, my dolly? Though it's the key to his whole character?"

"No! Why is it the key?"

"Because he was too proud," said H.M., "and he was far too conceited. He wouldn't demean himself in public by showin' he was concerned. He wouldn't admit that any man alive could take you away from the great Armand.

"Listen, my dolly, he never wanted to kill you! Neither did Aunt Hester. All they wanted to do was scare you so much that you'd run straight back to France. Don't you remember what you said yourself, in this office? I asked, 'Do you still want to stay at your Aunt Hester's?' And you cried out, 'No, but what else can I do except return to Paris?'—Got it now?"

"Then," Jenny blurted out, "just to get my dowry, this Armand has . . ."

"Oh, he wanted your money," said H.M. somberly. "But, towards the end, I don't think that was all. That murderous fight in the maze wasn't done altogether for money. I expect, in his own queer way, he was a little bit in love with you."

Again, since Jenny's eyes were clouding worse than ever, Tom intervened.

"But the locked room!" he said. "Where the gas-tap was turned on even while windows and door were both locked on the inside!"

"Well . . . now," H.M. sighed wearily. "I'd better tell you about it, because that locked room told me the whole ruddy truth before I even knew who was behind it.

"On the famous Night of Terrors," he added, pointing at Jenny, "you found, in your napkin at dinner, a note readin', 'You will die tonight, Jennifer.' Eh?"

"But who wrote the note?" interrupted Tom.

"Aunt Hester wrote it," snapped H.M. "There's never been much mystery about her. Her words and actions were too plain. She was the dominatin' character of her family, the only one, as I more than hinted, whom de Senneville bribed and prompted.

"After dinner," H.M. continued, still pointing at Jenny, "you went to your room at a little past eleven o'clock. One of the long windows, which you'd left closed, was now wide open. Correct?"

"Yes," said Jenny, and shuddered.

"You closed and locked the window again. You didn't need to touch or go near the gas fire. At shortly past twelve you went to bed, and soon fell asleep. The next thing you knew, Margot was bangin' on the door at six o'clock. A mysterious 'American' voice is asking what's wrong. They ran round to the window, pickin' up Uncle Fred on the way. Uncle Fred smashes the window. The mysterious 'American,' whom you can't see because you're too far gone, rushes over to the gas fire. He says, 'So-and-so, but it's turned full on!' And, apparently, he turns it off. Correct again?"

"Yes, yes."

"Not to me it isn't," said H.M., shaking his head. "Whoever this mysterious American was, he was the joker behind the trick. He told a flat lie. That gas *couldn't* have been turned full on."

"Why not?"

"Because you'd have been dead," H.M. said simply. "Let's suppose somebody, in the middle of the night, sneaks in and turns on the gas full-strength. Never mind what time it was. Let's even say it was as late, as impossibly late, as five o'clock in the morning. But there's no person in the world, breathing full-strength gas in an unventilated room, who can breathe it for an hour and still live. So I asked you a question to prove it."

"What question?"

"Oh, my dolly! You could describe every small noise you heard even when you were only half conscious. But you *didn't* hear any noise of a gas fire turned on full, which would have roared like a tornado. That's all."

"Oh!" exclaimed Jenny, caught up with a jolt. "Then . . . ?"

"Yes! Just before you retired to your room, Armand de Senneville—alias Steve Lamoreux—sneaked in and turned on the gas heater a tiny thread—only a tiny thread, not noticeable at all. He went out, leavin' the window wide open for good ventilation.

"You came in and closed the window. Well! What does happen, in very big rooms like that one, with such a tiny leak of gas? You can't hear it, you can't even smell it, for well over an hour. The bed is too far away. And it's caused tragedy before this. Meanwhile, for nearly six hours, the room is very slowly fillin' up with gas. When they found you, you were in just the condition I'd have expected.

"That's pretty much everything, my dolly. Armand de Senneville was lurkin' close outside, of course. You bet he was! He'd calculated his times, as he always does, but he was damned near too late to bust in himself, as he intended.

"He *had* to meet Margot—he couldn't help it. But that gal's a silly kind of wench, so excited she never wondered what he was doin' there. Uncle Fred barely noticed him. Later, it was easy for Aunt Hester to look 'em straight in the eye and tell 'em both they'd been dreaming. She was the only one who knew our Armand by sight. But, as for the 'miracle' of the locked room . . ."

"And that is all?" cried Jenny.

"Sure. What else did you expect?"

"I am disappoint!" suddenly exclaimed Jenny, hammering her fists on her knees. "I think this is a miracle. I think it cannot be solved. And then you show it is easy as eating sweets. Sir H.M., I hate you!"

The subsequent behavior of Sir Henry Merrivale, his martyrdom and his passionate addresses to the ceiling, is best left undescribed.

"So that's all the thanks I get, hey? They come to me and say, 'It's a miracle.' I say, 'It ain't,' and show 'em how it's done. Then they say, 'Oh, is that all? Silly old dummy! Stick him in the dustbin again.' "

It was fully half an hour before they smoothed him down.

"Very well!" he said, with a dark look at Jenny. "I'll not state what I think of some people. I'll just tell you what happened next and upset the whole apple cart. Aunt Hester had to drag a very sick and scared gal all the way to St. Paul's, so that Armand's hired ventriloquist could perform on time.

"But the apple cart was upset with an awful smash. 'Steve Lamoreux,' sittin' in the car just as he said he did, saw you run down the steps of St. Paul's and literally fall into this young feller's arms. When you went into the tea shop—well, Bob's your uncle. You bet he sneaked in and listened behind the partition. What he heard was just what he'd feared. You two were practically fallin' into each other's arms over the tea."

"I feel like this," Jenny confessed.

"I still feel like it," said Tom.

"Shut up," said the great man. "There were several courses open to 'Steve Lamoreux.' He chose the best, which was winnin' Tom Lockwood's confidence and stayin' close to him. So he deliberately sent this gal to me, supremely and conceitedly thinkin' the old goop would never see through *his* scheme.

"After Aunt Hester's row in the tea shop," here H.M. looked at Tom, "he went in and told his story. He more than won your confidence, son. He won your friendship."

"Yes," admitted Tom, and looked down at a closed fist. "He did."

"Of course, he couldn't go with you when you came to my office. He admitted the gal mustn't meet him. What he did is easy to guess. He followed you, and hung about in Horse Guards Avenue. D'ye know, I think I can see his face when we three piled downstairs and out to a police car, and I gave the address of his own hired ventriloquist.

"He got to the house about fifty seconds before we did, probably by waving a fiver in under a taxi-driver's nose. He nipped in by the back door, struck faster than a snake, and nipped out the same way while Johnson's body rolled down the front steps.

"And that tore it. As I said, the whole aspect of the business had changed.

"According to what I could deduce about the gas fire and the whispering gallery, *nobody* was actually trying to kill this gal. Somebody was trying to frighten her so much that she'd take the first plane back to Paris.

"Now who would be interested in doin' that, in conjunction with Aunt Hester? Who? You guess. And what about this odd 'American' or 'Canadian' who kept turning up all over the place without any explanation? Everybody promised to explain him; but nobody did."

H.M. pulled down his spectacles and glowered at Jenny over them.

"You see, my dolly, why I wanted you to go back to your aunt's house that night? You weren't in any real danger. And it wasn't likely somebody would try any games that night. If anything happened at all, it would happen during the expedition to Hampton Court next day—for one thing, Aunt Hester was far too insistent about takin' you there.

"And I could be there to stop it. And yet, burn me, I nearly missed it!"

The somber spectacles were now turned towards Tom.

"Son," observed H.M., "did you see the look on 'Steve Lamoreux's' face when you shouted along the path and asked this gal to marry you? And she said yes?"

"No, but I heard his voice. It was a voice I'd never heard him use before."

"Well! When it turned out you had tons of money and they couldn't accuse you of being a fortune hunter, did you notice him at any time after *that?*"

"Yes! His face was all pinched up and as pale as dough. But I thought—"

"Maybe you did. He had a knife with him, just in case. And that was the time he finally decided you were goin' to die."

Jenny pressed her face in her hands, and turned away.

"Oh, I was the villain!" said H.M. "In my role of guide, I wanted to see how Aunt Hester would act when she met Steve Lamoreux face to face. She behaved pretty well, but she couldn't keep her eyes from slidin' away when she mentioned the gal's fiancé.

"It was a silly-ass thing to do. I admit it. 'Cause I'd already made up my mind. That same day, since Armand de Senneville had been attached to the Yanks, I got his record and saw his photograph. To put the tin hat on it, 'Steve Lamoreux' had the star-gazin' cheek to walk into my office and spin his yarn.

"Even if I hadn't known already, the idiot gave himself away. He *would* smoke Yellow French cigarettes, and use sulphur matches. Even when he was very excited, he automatically held the match away from him until the sulphur had burned off—"

"Yes," interrupted Tom. "I saw him do that. But what about it?"

"Oh, son! He claimed he'd been in France only six months—"

"Yes, that's what he told me too!"

"And no foreigner on earth, after only six months in France, can get used to those sulphur matches. You always forget and swallow a lungful of sulphur. Only a Frenchman native-born automatically holds the match away for a few seconds. There, in my own office, was a Frenchman speakin' the most exquisite Yank.

"But you were the one in real danger, son. If I'd known beforehand you'd spent the night before prowlin' round this gal's windows with Armand de Senneville, I'd have had a fit. I repeat: he struck like a snake and killed poor old Johnson. Why? Just because he didn't want this gal to find out that it was *he* who was scaring her, or he'd lose her.

"Finally, last night at Hampton Court, I still don't know what funny business de Senneville, or Aunt Hester, or both of 'em, had planned. There wasn't time—the fireworks went up with a bang. I tried to keep you from goin' into that maze. Didn't you see me look round? Didn't you notice Lamoreux had slipped away? You dashed into the maze. He must have crawled up on top of it —we didn't see him enter—and followed you. But sometimes, for chivalrous young fools like you, there is mercy. You met the tough egg with his knife, and you knocked him flat. And that was the end."

There was a long silence, until Tom cleared his throat.

"H.M., what will they do to him?"

"Oh, they can't prove yet he killed Johnson. Not yet. In the meantime, he'll do a long stretch on two counts of attempted murder: with gas and with a knife. Then the coppers will snaffle him for killing Johnson. And he'll get what he deserves, son— he'll hang."

Jenny stood up suddenly, trembling. Tom put his arms around her, and held her tightly.

"It's all right!" he insisted. "Jenny, dear, it's all right!"

"Yes," said Jenny, holding him just as tightly, "but that is why you must not leave me, ever. It is all right—*now!*"

For once in his life, Sir Henry Merrivale did not roar out about canoodling in his office. Slowly, somberly, he got up from his chair and wandered over to one of the windows. There, his hands folded behind his back, he stood looking out over the river and the mighty curve of London.

Format by Gayle A. Jaeger
Set in Linotype Electra
Composed by York Composition Co., Inc.
Printed by York Composition Co., Inc.
Bound by The Haddon Craftsmen, Inc.
HARPER & ROW, PUBLISHERS, INCORPORATED